Psychic on the Rocks

Midlife Magic Cocktail Club, Book 4

Copyright © 2021 by Annabel Chase

All rights reserved.

No part of this book may be reproduced in any form or by any electronic or mechanical means, including information storage and retrieval systems, without written permission from the author, except for the use of brief quotations in a book review.

Cover by Mayflower Studio

❈ Created with Vellum

# CHAPTER ONE

Rebecca Angelos held up her phone to share the screen with the pug currently seated on her lap. "What do you think, Elvis? There's something shifty about his eyes, I think." She swiped left and regarded the next profile with more interest. "He has a nice smile."

Elvis barked, prompting Rebecca to swipe right. Nothing happened. No ping! to indicate he'd already swiped right on her. Maybe he just hadn't seen her profile yet.

She set down the phone and sighed. Who was she kidding? He'd probably swiped left on her multiple times already. Why go for a woman her age when he could still be pulling from the thirty-five to thirty-nine age bracket? If a man wasn't smart enough to recognize what a middle-aged woman had to offer, then Rebecca didn't want him anyway.

"I have that lunch date with Tony coming up," she told Elvis, "so it's not like I'm desperate." She hadn't met Tony in person yet; they'd only chatted online. Dating was a lot like house hunting though. You could look at dozens of beautiful photos of the house online, but the moment you pulled into the driveway to see it in person, you'd know whether you could picture yourself living there.

Slobber dripped from Elvis's jowls onto her wrist and she deftly wiped away the droplets with a spare cloth. When you worked around animals all day every day, you knew how to be prepared. Maybe she would never be one of those women with a tote bag the size of Connecticut that stored every known need from Band-Aids to juice boxes, but Rebecca could whip out a squeaky toy and a liver treat at a moment's notice. She was childless by choice and perfectly content to play surrogate mom to a shelter filled with furry friends in need of homes.

"No good," Iago squawked. Rebecca glanced across the room at the parrot on his perch in the deluxe birdcage.

"Who's no good?" Rebecca held up the phone for the parrot. "This guy?"

"No good," Iago repeated.

Iago, along with all his accoutrements, had been left at the shelter six months ago by a weeping woman named Shelley. Iago had lived with Shelley's mother until the older woman moved into a nursing home and, sadly, the parrot had to go. Shelley lived in an apartment that didn't allow pets and was unable to take the parrot, which filled her with guilt. She'd managed to go through almost an entire box of tissues before she left the shelter. Rebecca had assured her a dozen times that Iago would be fine and he was. Rebecca had grown accustomed to the parrot's random remarks. Sometimes he cocked his brightly colored head to the side when she spoke, as though listening to every word intently.

Not to be outdone by Iago, Elvis barked. The pug had been a resident of the shelter for almost a year now and Rebecca worried that he'd never find his forever home. He was a pleasure to be around, but he had a couple of medical issues that made his care more labor intensive and, thus, more expensive to adopt. As much as she wanted to place him in a good home, she was perfectly content to have him with her at the shelter. He was always good company and, even better, seemed to have a sixth sense when it came to dating profiles. Elvis had shown his approval of Tony by licking the screen.

Rebecca set Elvis on the floor and puttered across the room to check on the latest arrival. The domestic shorthaired cat was in reasonable shape, for which Rebecca was grateful. Some arrivals weren't so lucky and required immediate medical attention.

Rebecca peered into the enclosure. "How are you, buddy?"

The cat gazed at her with a sleepy expression. At least he didn't seem distressed about his unfamiliar environment. The cat had been found in a box on the side of a highway by a man on his way home from a business trip. No collar or microchip. A cat toy in the shape of a fish and a small container of food had been left inside the box as well. Someone had cared enough to do that much, but not enough to surrender the cat to a safe location. If there was one thing Rebecca had learned in her forty-seven years, it was that people made questionable choices.

She hadn't yet decided on a name. Sometimes a name came to her immediately, yet other times it took weeks before the right name stuck. Unfortunately many of the animals had plenty of time at the shelter to receive a new name. She wished it were different. Just like children, they deserved a home where they were loved.

Rebecca peered through the doorway into the next room, which housed the majority of the shelter's animals. It would be time to stretch their legs soon. They were taken in shifts, big dogs first. Sometimes, when she was outside in the courtyard surrounded by animals with beams of sunlight shining down on them and birds tweeting overhead, she felt like the Snow White of Shelters. If only the animals cooked and cleaned—she'd be set for life.

She checked the clock on her phone. Peaches was due to arrive any minute. The twenty-year-old was one of several volunteers who rotated shifts throughout the week. There was no way Rebecca could do it all on her own. She'd only become the director six months ago, although she'd worked at the shelter for years. When Ida had announced she was retiring and moving to Arizona to avoid any more Pocono winters, Rebecca had been crushed. Not only that, but she'd worried about the future of Cloverleaf Critters. Ida had been the founder and served as the director for a decade and Rebecca wasn't sure she was ready to step into her mentor's shoes. Rebecca wasn't a leader like Ida. She was a workhorse by nature, preferring a low-level role, yet here she was. In charge. When her friend Kate told her she suffered from imposter syndrome, Rebecca had looked up the term. As far she was concerned, it wasn't accurate because she *was* a fraud. She didn't belong in this role, but she was the only one committed enough to take it on and there was no way she would leave the animals in the lurch.

Still peering through the doorway, Rebecca made eye contact with Simon in his enclosure and couldn't resist crossing the room to greet him. She'd found the kitten behind a dumpster in town. She didn't know whether he'd been abandoned by the mother or something bad had happened to her to prevent her coming back. Either way, Simon had been in dire need of care that included hand-rearing. He was thriving at the shelter, which pleased Rebecca. She only wished someone would come along who recognized his wonderful qualities and chose to adopt him. Soon.

"You're looking so handsome today, Simon," she said,

stroking his head. He was an extremely affectionate cat and any human would be lucky to have him as a companion. Maybe she would highlight him at the next Senior Night. She'd resisted the urge so far because she wasn't sure the seniors were ready for a spry kitten like Simon. He'd mellowed in recent weeks, though, and she thought it might be a good time to showcase him. Senior Night was a monthly program that Rebecca had developed with Ida's approval that involved matching animals with senior citizens. The shelter also provided subsidies for those residents who might benefit from companionship but who couldn't otherwise afford the care or adoption fees.

The thought of Senior Night reminded her that she needed to ask her friends to swap their usual cocktail club evening. Peaches had accidentally scheduled Rebecca's animal adoption talk at the library for the same evening and it was easier to move cocktail club than a public event.

As she picked up her phone to text the group, the screen lit up with an incoming call. Duty called, literally.

"Hey, Beth. How are you?" Beth was one of the shelter's foster moms. Rebecca had lost count of the number of animals Beth had successfully fostered for the shelter. "Is Clyde working out okay? Any problems?"

"That's why I'm calling, actually," Beth said.

Rebecca's stomach dropped. She hoped there wasn't an issue with Clyde. The dog seemed affable enough and Beth was adept at gaining the trust and affection of even the most difficult animals.

"No, no problem at all. It's good news. Gary and I have decided that we'd like to adopt him. I hope that's okay."

Rebecca's spirits soared. She loved nothing more than to match an animal with a loving home and Beth's was definitely that. "That's terrific. I'm so pleased to hear it. I'll get started on the paperwork right away."

She was still smiling when Beth added, "Unfortunately that means we're not going to be able to take anymore foster animals."

Rebecca grimaced. "That's too bad."

"Gary has vowed to divorce me if I don't stick to the deal. It's the only reason he agreed to let us adopt Clyde."

A double-edged sword. Because of course it was. "Well, I'm thrilled for you. This is still great news."

By the time Rebecca hung up the phone, her good mood had dissipated. Good foster homes were always in short supply and she'd been able to rely on Beth. As elated as she was for sweet Clyde to have found a good home, it would be a loss for the shelter.

Returning to the counter, she shot off a text to the other members of the cocktail club about switching to tonight. If they couldn't change their schedules last minute, she'd have to miss a week. Not the end of the world, although she'd be disappointed. The four friends met weekly to enjoy drinks and have a few laughs. There'd been five of them until Inga's death nearly a year ago. The older woman had been an inspiration to Rebecca. As the club's founder, Inga Paulsen had been the one to invite Rebecca to join. Not a day went by that Rebecca didn't think of her. Although they'd known each other only a few years, she'd had a profound effect on Rebecca's life. Inga was the kind of woman who'd lived life to the fullest and sparked joy in everyone she met.

Rebecca was never going to be like Inga. She didn't have that kind of personality. That was one of the reasons she was more comfortable at the shelter than she was at a cocktail party. Animals were easier to navigate and she didn't have to admonish herself later for saying something stupid. There was also something to be said for showing up to work at a place where everyone liked you.

Well, most of the animals liked her. There was the occasional anomaly, but Rebecca usually managed to win them over. Who needed a date on Saturday night when she had her choice of cuddle buddies both at home and work?

The door burst open and Peaches appeared wearing what looked to Rebecca like a burgundy infant romper with the image of an origami dragon on the front. The twenty-year-old's blonde hair was styled in two thick braids and she'd changed her nose ring from a gold stud to a small silver hoop.

"Hey, Peaches."

Peaches took a step forward and halted. "Ooh."

"What's wrong?"

Peaches looked from left to right. "I don't know. Do you feel it?"

"No good," Iago squawked.

Peaches inclined her head toward the parrot. "What he said." She shrugged off her backpack. "I think we need to see what the cards have to say."

Rebecca headed for the doorway. "The cards will have to wait because the dogs can't anymore."

The buzzer sounded at the entrance and Rebecca looked up as the door opened and an unfamiliar man entered. He had a thick head of salt-and-pepper hair and wore the kind of suit that would have looked more at home on a city banker. A few of the dogs immediately started howling as though finding his scent disagreeable. Rebecca didn't trust anybody that set off multiple dogs at once. The animals were the best security system a person could have.

"I'll get started," Peaches said. She ducked into the adjoining room and closed the door to stifle the noise.

"Welcome to Cloverleaf Critters," Rebecca said, maintaining a friendly demeanor. "How can I help you?" He was probably here to adopt a puppy for his much younger girlfriend. Or his mistress. A furry friend to keep her company while he was unable to devote attention to her. Needless to say, Rebecca took an instant dislike to him.

"My name is Brian Shea." He stood at the counter observing her. He seemed to be waiting for a flicker of recognition. When none was forthcoming, he continued, "I'm the owner of this building. Shea Properties."

Rebecca shook off her surprise. "Oh, I'm sorry Mr. Shea. We haven't met." She offered her hand. "I'm Rebecca Angelos, the director here."

"Yes, I remember seeing the note from Ida that there would be a change in leadership."

"What brings you in today?" The monthly lease payments were taken from the bank account automatically so she knew the shelter wasn't in arrears.

He surveyed the interior. "I'm here as a courtesy, to give you notice that I've decided to sell the building. When the lease is up, you'll have to find other accommodation for the animals."

Rebecca's mouth opened and she suddenly found it difficult to breathe. "When the lease ends, as in six weeks from now?"

He didn't meet her gaze. Instead he walked the length of the room, stopping to examine the chipped paint on the wall. "Check your email. I've had my assistant send over written notice as per the lease agreement, but I thought I'd take a look at the state of the place before I start bringing buyers through."

Rebecca's throat went dry and she had trouble forming words. He was selling the building. This building. Right out from under her.

She pulled herself together. "Is there a particular reason you've decided to sell, Mr. Shea? We've been making our payments on time. We're a good tenant."

He barely glanced at her, currently intent on a few nicks

on the doorframe. "It's just business, Rebecca. Surely you can understand that."

She bristled at the use of her first name. She could tell from that brief exchange that respect was only one way.

"The market is booming in the downtown area and I've decided to take advantage of it." He thrust his hands into his trouser pockets and stopped at Iago's cage to peer at the parrot. "I didn't realize you took in birds."

"We take in any animal that needs a home," she said. "Right now we have a bearded dragon, two ferrets, and two bunnies. We once had a dog-wolf hybrid, but she outgrew the space so we were able to get her a place at a sanctuary." That had been a harrowing experience. Rebecca and Ida had worked tirelessly to secure a home for the animal who'd grown much too large to remain at the shelter.

He motioned to the doorway. "Can I go in there and look around or do you need to lock away any animals first?"

"Be my guest, but I can't promise they'll let you walk around in peace and quiet." Peaches would be in the courtyard with some of the bigger dogs by now. That would help keep the noise level down.

He opened the door and Rebecca thought it best to accompany him, just in case he decided to walk too close to an enclosure. Brian Shea gave off an unpleasant vibe that some of the animals seemed to have already picked up on.

"I'm surprised how clean this place is considering the number of animals living here," he said, after a brief inspection. "What's that white room used for? It looks like a surgical suite."

"That's because the vet uses it to perform surgeries on the days he's here," Rebecca said. "He doesn't work for the shelter, but we have a contract with him."

"I didn't realize you handled that sort of thing right here in the building." He barely glanced at the animals. Rebecca wasn't sure how a person walked past all those sweet faces without pausing to gush over at least one of them. Brian Shea was clearly some sort of cyborg.

"We do what we have to do," she said vaguely.

"June 30th isn't too far away," he said. "If I were you, I'd start looking now or you won't find another lease in time. It's not like this is a typical office setup."

No kidding. Thanks for the mansplaining, cyborg.

He sniffed the air. "Is there anything that can be done about the smell?"

Rebecca frowned. "What smell?"

"It smells like a barn."

Rebecca bit back a snarky reply. "We'll be sure to air out the space before any showings."

"Good idea. I'll be in touch," he said, exiting the room.

Rebecca stared at the empty space where he'd been standing and prayed to the universe that she was having a horrible daydream—because relocating the shelter would be an absolute nightmare.

# CHAPTER TWO

"Way to go, Rebecca," she muttered to herself. Leave it to her to run the shelter into the ground after Ida had entrusted it to her. The older woman should have known better. Rebecca wasn't equipped to handle a crisis. It was one of the reasons she'd been perfectly fine with not having children. She knew herself well enough to realize that she wouldn't make a very good mother. She had no patience with people, although she acknowledged she had endless patience with animals. It took the better part of a year to gain Sienna's trust, but Rebecca had persevered. The husky had been surrendered by a neglectful owner and had taken a long time to adjust to a loving environment. Sienna now lived with a local family with two teenagers. She wasn't a good fit for young children, but Rebecca had known instinctively that the Lopez family was the right one for Sienna.

She silently fumed as she and Peaches finished another round of courtyard visits with the animals. She didn't tell Peaches the details of her conversation with Brian Shea. Although the young woman was intuitive enough to recognize there was a problem, Rebecca was relieved she had the good sense not to pry. Rebecca needed time to process and right now she had too many immediate tasks to complete.

As she returned to the counter, her phone lit up with a call from her mother. Finally. Rebecca had called three days ago. "Hi Mom."

"Hello Rebecca. I just remembered I had a voicemail from you."

Ah, yes. Her daughter, the afterthought. Typical.

Rebecca could hear the rush of wind through the phone. "Are you on a walk?"

"Yes, your father and I are taking advantage of the nice spring weather and walking the perimeter of the pond."

Rebecca shouldn't have been surprised. Her mother always seemed to squeeze her in rather than make her a priority. It had been this way for as long as Rebecca could remember. More than once she'd thought her parents shouldn't have bothered to reproduce when they were obviously more than content with each other.

"Sounds nice. It's overcast here." Rebecca's parents lived in central New Jersey. Although the town was only about a ninety-minute drive, they rarely came to visit. They seemed to enjoy their busy retirement schedule.

"Is that why you called?" her mother asked. "To update me on the weather?"

Rebecca felt a familiar ache in her chest. "No. I thought you'd want to know I was able to find someone to adopt the cat I told you about."

Her mother paused. "Which cat was it? You mention so many. I don't remember."

Rebecca closed her eyes. "The one with the missing leg."

"Oh, right. Well, that's good news. Listen, before I forget, your father and I were thinking we'd come for a visit the week after Memorial Day."

Rebecca straightened from her slouched position. "Really?"

"Unless you have plans. Maybe a new boyfriend?"

Rebecca rubbed her temple. "No, Mom. No special plans. I would love it if you and Dad came."

"Will you be able to keep those animals of yours sequestered?"

Rebecca couldn't bite her tongue when it came to her furry companions. "The animals live with me and it will be easy enough to maneuver around them."

Her parents hadn't been pet people. As a child, Rebecca briefly had a rabbit, but the animal had proven too much work and was sent packing—to where, Rebecca never knew.

"I'll be sure to leave my black clothes at home," her mother said.

"Or you could bring a lint brush," Rebecca suggested. She had her own stash of them, of course, but she was in the mood to make a point.

"Yes, I think I will." Her mother said something unintelligible to her father. "We've run into some friends from the clubhouse. Talk later, okay?"

"Okay, bye." Rebecca turned the phone facedown on the counter, annoyed. Why should this conversation be different from any other one with her parents? There was always someone better or more interesting to talk to than Rebecca.

"Way to go," the parrot squawked. "So stupid."

Rebecca gaped at the parrot. "Who taught you to speak?" It occurred to her the parrot only repeated what he heard. For a fleeting moment, Rebecca worried that one of the volunteers had been speaking too harshly to the animals until the parrot's words settled in her mind. No, these words were familiar and not because they were the words of volunteers. These were Rebecca's words she sometimes directed at herself out loud when no one was around to overhear her.

No one except Iago.

Her cheeks grew flushed at the realization. She quickly brushed it off and continued with her routine. No point in dwelling on the negative. She obviously did plenty of that without noticing it.

By the time the next volunteer arrived for her shift, Rebecca was back to worrying about the visit from Brian Shea. What if she couldn't find a suitable location in time? Cloverleaf Critters was a safe haven for the rejected and unwanted animals in the area. Without the shelter, there would be nowhere for these animals to go. Its closure could result in problems with animal control and an increase in euthanasia cases. The mere prospect made Rebecca's blood boil. She could try to find other shelters to take them, but that would be tough and it would still leave a gaping hole in the community.

Cloverleaf Critters filled a need, whether people realized it or not. They were a no-kill shelter. If they closed, she would have to find homes for each and every animal before it was too late. If they couldn't do that on a regular basis, how could she do it under a looming deadline? Even if she could get the current group of animals adopted, that was only a temporary solution. There would always be more. Rebecca stretched her neck from side to side and tried to calm herself through deep breathing. She had to keep a clear head and come up with a plan. She just had no idea what that plan would be.

She was grateful when it was finally time to head home. A warm bath with scented lavender soap would help her decompress and, if that didn't work, the cocktails would. She was relieved her friends could switch to tonight at such late notice. She needed their company right now more than they knew.

As she left the downtown area, fat droplets of rain

splashed on the windshield and she wiped them away. To make matters worse, Rebecca saw signs for roadwork ahead that hadn't been there this morning. A long line of cars stretched in front of her, moving at a snail's pace. Terrific. If the drive took too long, she'd have to forgo the bath.

Rebecca was surprised by the amount of traffic on the road. Then again, they were heading into tourist season once again. The closer they got to Memorial Day, the more visitors Lake Cloverleaf would receive. The population would balloon during the height of the summer months. Although it was a pain for year-round residents, Rebecca recognized that the influx of tourists meant much-needed money for many of the local businesses. Her friend Julie was finally getting her family home up and running as a B&B and the summer months would be crucial to her first year of business. She was excited to see what the future had in store for her friend.

Rebecca felt a momentary pang of misery at the thought of Julie. At the start of the new year, Julie had received her gift from the dearly departed Inga—the ability to see and communicate with ghosts. According to Ethan Townsend, Inga's lawyer and Libbie's boyfriend, Inga had been a witch who'd divided her magical assets among the four remaining friends. They'd been given a seemingly empty jar and four blank books and sent on their merry way.

*Witches are created, not born*, they'd been told.

Initially Rebecca hadn't known how to take the information. It seemed far-fetched and yet if any woman was a witch with a magical inheritance to leave behind, it was Inga. Rebecca had half expected the spry eighty-five-year-old to pop out of her casket and do the Macarena.

They'd left the meeting with Ethan and gathered around the empty jar to open it. Along with the stench of garlic, there'd been a…sensation. Soon afterward, a cocktail recipe had appeared on the first page of Libbie's book. It seemed that the magical cocktail recipes manifested when the time was right for each woman to receive her gift.

Apparently the time would never be right for Rebecca, as she was the only one who'd yet to receive her gift.

Rebecca knew it was silly to feel left out. She'd been last to be invited to join the cocktail club. Naturally she would be last to inherit her assets. It wasn't as though she'd done anything to deserve the windfall. She wasn't as accomplished as Kate, or as sweet and well-intentioned as Libbie, and she certainly wasn't as kindhearted as Julie who'd suffered a terrible loss when her husband died three years ago. Rebecca was an afterthought and that was okay with her. At least she'd been included.

Desperate to squeeze in a bath before cocktail club, she turned off the main road and set her GPS to take her home via an alternate route. The rain chose that moment to intensify and she could barely see through the sheet of water. Great. She tended to stick to the main roads and wasn't as familiar with some of the back roads, although with her luck the GPS would lose the signal.

She slowed the car to a crawl as the GPS put her on one of the narrow roads with no shoulder that wound its way up the mountain in a snakelike pattern. She was relieved when the computer voice told her to turn left ahead, although there was every chance the next road would be worse. She knew she had a flashlight, a map, and an envelope of emergency cash in the glove compartment like her dad had taught her. Did she also have an emergency patch kit and a spare tire in her trunk? Rebecca had no idea. She simply had to hope there were no rusty nails in her path, not that she'd spot them. Her windshield wipers were swishing left and right so fast, she worried they'd break and fly off.

As she prepared to turn left, she noticed a house set back

about half a mile from the road. It wasn't the house she noticed as much as the dog in the yard. She could tell at a glance the Doberman was malnourished, but the sight of the chain fastened to his neck set her teeth on edge. The pickup truck in the driveway forced her hand. If someone was home and had left the dog outside in torrential rain, she couldn't let it pass.

She swerved into the driveway, her tires squealing with the snap decision. She heard the crunch of gravel beneath her as she drove the length of the driveway and parked behind the truck. The dog was too subdued to bother barking. He regarded her with a vacant expression that tugged at her heartstrings.

Pellets of rain smacked her face she exited the car, but she was only vaguely aware of the sensation. She was too focused on the dog and his evident misery. Looking at him now and seeing the evidence of his mistreatment shook her to her core. She spared a glance over her shoulder at the squat white house with its broken shutters and torn screen door. Her inner voice tried to persuade her to leave.

*These people aren't going to listen to you. Go get someone who can help.*

Rebecca stood frozen in place, feeling torn. She had contact numbers for the right people, but no one would come out tonight. What if something happened to the dog between now and the time when someone came to the house? Rebecca would never forgive herself. This dog required immediate attention. On the other hand, Rebecca didn't feel capable of handling the situation. She was a petite woman alone in a rural area with spotty cell reception. What did she think she was going to accomplish all by herself? Her voice wouldn't matter to these people.

"Hey, buddy." She crouched a safe distance from the dog

and looked into his eyes. All she saw was sadness reflected back at her.

She resumed an upright position, her decision made. "I'm going to try my best to get you out of here."

This dog needed her. She turned and marched up to the front door, her body shaking with adrenaline and anger. She knew she had to maintain a calm demeanor and resisted the urge to be confrontational. She'd read plenty of articles on the subject of removing a dog from a bad situation, but her rescues didn't involve demanding to take a dog from an existing owner. Usually the animals were either found or voluntarily surrendered to the shelter.

She rapped on the door loudly, letting her fist release its violent energy on the door rather than where she wanted to put it. The interior door jerked open and a man squinted at her. He wore a baseball hat and a flimsy white tank top with jeans that hung too low on his waist. The moment he opened the screen door, Rebecca smelled stale beer on his breath. She swallowed hard. Too late to turn back now.

"You lost or something?" he demanded, eyeing her with a suspicious glint.

"No, sir." Rebecca made sure that her voice sounded confident and friendly. "I was checking to see whether anyone was home. Your dog's outside and the rain's gotten pretty bad."

His gaze flicked toward the cowering dog and back to her. "None of your business now, is it?"

"No, of course not," she said. "It's just that I was passing by and noticed he was outside and thought maybe I could offer some help to make him more comfortable."

The man scowled. "It's a dog," he said, as though that explained everything.

"Yes, I realize that. I happen to work with animals and I

can tell by looking at him that he might be in need of medical attention."

The man sniffed loudly. "Do I look like I have money for vet bills?"

Rebecca mustered her courage. "I understand your situation, sir. Having a pet is a huge responsibility. They can require so much money and time." She glanced at the dog, the misery emanating from his emaciated body. She couldn't leave this property without the dog or she'd never forgive herself.

"You don't need to tell me that," he said.

"You know, maybe you'd be happier if the dog was rehomed with someone in a position to pay for things like vet bills. I don't mean to overstep, but I would be more than happy to take him off your hands if you'd be willing to surrender him." Rebecca wanted to shut her eyes in an effort to block out her discomfort, but she forced herself to maintain eye contact with the man. She watched his expression shift from annoyance to consideration and hope bloomed in her heart.

"I feel like if you're going to take my dog, you need to compensate me for it. I paid a lot of money to take care of it over the years."

"How old is he?" she asked. The more information she could get now, the better.

The man scratched the back of his head. "Maybe three? It belonged to my last girlfriend, but she left without it. I set it loose once, but the dumb thing came back. Don't even know when it ain't wanted."

Rebecca bristled at his response. She didn't bother to ask what the dog's name was. Whatever the name had been, the dog would require a new name now, one that didn't fill the dog with dread whenever he heard it. She wouldn't be surprised to learn he'd been beaten.

"How much would you take for him?"

He appeared to mull it over. "Fifty bucks ought to do it."

Rebecca racked her brain and tried to remember whether she had any cash in the car. Relief flooded her when she remembered the emergency envelope with cash in the glove compartment.

"I think I might be able to swing it," Rebecca said. "Let me run back to my car." She dashed to the passenger-side door before he could change his mind and demand a higher price. She wouldn't put it past him. She rifled through the glove compartment as fast as she could and plucked two twenties and a ten from the envelope. She ran back to the front door and thrust the cash into his outstretched hand. Normally when someone surrendered an animal, she would ask for paperwork to be signed, but she knew it wouldn't be a problem. This man would be happy to see the back end of the dog.

He counted the money and closed the door without another word. Turning toward the dog, Rebecca wiped the rain from her eyes. She'd handled enough dogs to know what to do next.

Once the Doberman was settled on the spare blanket across the backseat, Rebecca reversed out of the driveway, her heart pounding. She debated whether to go back to the shelter. In the end, she decided the dog was better off at her house for the night. She'd leave a voicemail for Dr. Nate and ask him to swing by in the morning. In the meantime, she would do her best to make the dog comfortable. Considering what he'd likely gone through, the Doberman didn't exhibit any aggressive behavior. Bless his sweet heart.

By the time she arrived home, the rain had subsided and sunlight streamed through the clouds. She hoped it was a promise of things to come because they certainly couldn't get much worse.

# CHAPTER THREE

"Thank you so much for coming here tonight instead," Rebecca said, greeting her friends as they came through the door.

"We all have a kink in the schedule every now and again," Kate acknowledged. "When I left, Lucas had ribbons in his hair courtesy of Ava, so I can't wait to see the finished product when I get home."

Rebecca couldn't help but smile. Kate Golden had been the definition of a perfectionist until recent events encouraged her to ease up on herself. Rebecca had always liked Kate, hard edges and all, but she could tell her friend was much happier and more accepting of herself now. Whereas before the blonde radiated confidence, she now radiated contentment too.

"Was I supposed to bring snacks?" Libbie asked, observing the empty counter space in the kitchen.

"No, no. I'm running behind, that's all." Rebecca had forsaken her own bath for the Doberman's and ended up with barely enough time to change her clothes before their arrival.

Kate opened the fridge and pulled out a container of cheese. "This works for me."

"Any Pop-Tarts?" Julie asked.

Rebecca opened the pantry door. "No, but I have Wheat Thins to go with the cheese."

"Bring it," Julie said.

"If we don't already have an itinerary tonight, I've been messing around with a few cocktail recipes." Libbie produced her magical recipe book from her tote bag and flicked through the pages. Rebecca winced at the sight of all the recipes, knowing her own pages were still blank. She quickly squelched the pity party. Libbie deserved to have magic in her life; this wasn't about Rebecca.

Julie peered over Libbie's shoulder to scan the prospective recipes. "I'm in the mood for a lighter drink. It's the warmer weather we've been having. Makes me want to stick a paper umbrella in something fruity."

"I brought my book tonight too," Kate said. "I've been fine-tuning a few mocktail recipes. I even brought my own ingredients." She emptied the contents of the bag onto the counter.

"Of course you did," Rebecca said. "I have lemons here, you know. I'm not completely uncivilized."

Julie laughed as she reached into her bag and pulled out her recipe book, setting it on the counter beside the other two. "Great minds think alike."

Rebecca rolled her eyes. "Well, let me get mine so I don't feel completely left out." She spun on her heel and retrieved the book from the cabinet next to the refrigerator. "Let me see. Which one shall I choose? Like my dating prospects, there are just too many options. I'm spoiled for choice." With exaggerated motions, she opened the book on the counter and flipped to the first page.

Her heart skipped a beat.

There on the first page of the book was a recipe where none had been before.

"I have a recipe," she said, so quietly that no one else heard her.

The other women continued talking about their own suggestions for the evening.

"I have a recipe," she said, more loudly this time.

The other three women turned to face her.

"A recipe?" Libbie echoed.

Rebecca tapped the page with a shaky index finger. "Look."

"When did that happen?" Kate asked, peering at the page.

"I don't know. It's not like I check every day." Only every few days, not that she would admit it out loud.

Julie fixed her with a penetrating gaze. "Can you think of anything that happened that might have triggered it?"

"Has anything strange happened to you?" Libbie added.

"Nothing strange would've happened yet," Kate said. "She needs to drink the cocktail first."

Rebecca didn't need to replay recent events in her mind to know the triggering event. "I think it has something to do with the Doberman I rescued."

"What Doberman?" Julie asked.

Rebecca turned her gaze toward the guest bedroom where the dog was currently ensconced. "He's the reason I was late getting home." She told them about her earlier detour and the encounter with the dog's owner.

Libbie gasped. "Rebecca, you could've been killed. You have no idea what kind of man he was. He could've turned a gun on you."

"I know, but I couldn't walk away and leave the dog in such a horrible situation. Dr. Nate will examine him first thing in the morning at the shelter, but he's staying the night here."

"That was very brave," Julie said.

*Or very stupid*, Rebecca thought to herself. Either way, the deed was done and she and the dog were both fine. A lucky escape.

"I guess this means we know what your first cocktail will be tonight," Kate said, tapping the page. "Do you have the ingredients you need?"

Rebecca reviewed the instructions. "Lemon juice."

"Ha! No worries. I've got you covered." Kate rolled the lemon across the counter. "One unwaxed organic lemon coming up."

Julie snickered. "Is there anything you don't cart around in that mom bag of yours?"

"Chris Hemsworth, not that I would object," Kate said, smiling.

Libbie glanced at the empty tote bag. "In that case, you're going to need a bigger bag."

Rebecca's attention was still on the recipe. "I need lavender, hibiscus, and echinacea." She laughed. "I guess the universe thinks I have a cold."

Libbie peered over her shoulder. "Echinacea clears blockages. Maybe you have a spiritual blockage that needs clearing."

"That makes sense," Kate chimed in. "I remember reading that echinacea opens psychic channels."

Julie clapped her hands. "I'm so excited. I can't wait to see what happens next."

Rebecca cast a sidelong glance at her. "On that note, how are your visions these days?" Rebecca was glad she hadn't been on the receiving end of that particular gift. The only bumps she wanted to hear in the night were the ones involving the cats jumping from one dresser surface to another.

Julie leaned a hip against the island. "Not too intrusive

lately. It seems to have calmed down now, which is good timing because most of my focus has been geared toward getting the B&B up and running."

"You're just in time for prime season," Kate said. "Your website looks amazing, by the way. I was stalking it earlier today."

Julie beamed with pride. "Thanks. This whole thing has been so much more fun than I anticipated. I mean, it's work, but I'm really enjoying the process."

"That's great," Rebecca said. That was one thing she could say for herself as well. Rebecca absolutely loved what she did every day. She wouldn't trade the animals at Cloverleaf Critters for anything in the world, which was why the news from Brian Shea was so upsetting.

Kate seemed to notice her change in expression. "What's the matter, Rebecca?"

Rebecca silently chastised herself for drawing attention away from Julie's good news. She didn't want to be the Debbie Downer of the group. She preferred to keep her negative thoughts to herself because she didn't want to risk alienating the best friends she'd ever had. If they realized what she was really like, they might decide she wasn't worth their time and attention anymore.

Rebecca forced a cheerful smile. "It's nothing. Just worried about the dog." She felt guilty for withholding the information about the sale of the building, but she thought it was best to keep it under wraps for now. Maybe some miracle would occur and she wouldn't have to tell anyone. She felt responsible, as though this news was somehow her fault. Then again, Rebecca had a tendency to take all failures personally.

Kate opened a drawer and retrieved a knife. "Let's get started on this cocktail for Rebecca."

Julie nudged her gently. "Looks like Inga saved the best for last."

Rebecca smiled but said nothing. More like the other way around.

"How can we get started without the ingredients?" Rebecca asked. "The rest aren't things I keep in the house."

Libbie pulled out her phone and typed a quick text. "Your ingredients will be here in approximately fifteen minutes. I'm sure we can keep ourselves occupied until then."

Kate angled her head toward Libbie's phone. "You used your thumbs to text. When did that start? Last time I saw you text, it was index fingers in slow motion."

"The kids were mocking me," Libbie said. "It was adapt or perish."

Julie wiggled her fingers. "I can't do it. I have arthritis starting between my thumb and index finger and texting like that would aggravate it."

"You also don't have two teenagers mocking your every text, so I think you'll be fine," Libbie pointed out.

"Who's bringing the herbs over?" Rebecca asked.

"Courtney knows where they are, so she's getting them for Ethan and he's driving over with them." Libbie shrugged. "It takes a village."

Rebecca stared at her in amazement. She could never be as together as her friends, not in a million years. It was a wonder they tolerated her.

"Why don't we do our compliment circle while we wait?" Kate suggested. "We can start with prosecco." She patted the top of the bottle she'd set on the island, along with the other contents of her bag.

Rebecca groaned inwardly. She wasn't in the mood for compliments. Then again, she rarely was.

"Good idea," Libbie said.

Kate popped the lid off a bottle and poured the bubbly liquid into four flutes.

"I'll start," Julie said. "Libbie, you're a wizard for pulling together the ingredients Rebecca needs at a moment's notice. Kate, your confidence gives me confidence even when I don't feel capable. Rebecca, you've inspired a love of animals I didn't even know I had."

"And one for yourself," Kate said.

Julie appeared thoughtful. "I'm an example of never being too old to start over."

"Cheers to that," Kate said, raising her flute. "I'll go next. Julie, your strength has been an inspiration to us all. I'm so impressed with everything you've done with the B&B and I know it's going to be a huge success." She pivoted toward Libbie. "Watching you raise Courtney and Josh makes me want to be a better mother."

A whimper escaped Libbie and she threw an arm around Kate's slender shoulders, planting a wet kiss on her cheek.

Kate's gaze flicked to Rebecca. "If I ever needed someone to fight in my corner, you'd be the first person I'd call. The animals in this town don't know how lucky they are, but we do."

Rebecca felt a rush of guilt. The animals wouldn't feel so lucky when they found themselves homeless again. They'd wish Ida was still in charge.

"And I'm a strong woman with an endless supply of energy that I use to lift others instead of bringing them down," Kate continued.

"Damn straight," Rebecca said.

Libbie cleared her throat. "Kate, you're a supernova, as always. Julie, you are the physical embodiment of love and devotion and I can't think of anyone more suited to serve as a messenger of the spirits."

"Lorraine might take issue with that opinion," Julie joked.

Lorraine was a psychic witch that referred to herself as the Messenger of the Spirits, among other things. She was what people referred to as 'a real character.'

"Rebecca, you're the lighthouse in a storm and I have mastered texting with my thumbs which is something I never thought possible," Libbie continued.

"That's lame," Kate said.

Libbie glared at her. "This is a no judgment compliment circle, remember?"

"Your turn, Rebecca," Julie said.

Rebecca had secretly hoped they'd forget and move on. Fat chance. She didn't mind giving them compliments, but she wasn't in the mindset to give one to herself.

"Kate, when the world demands lemonade, you supply the lemons. Libbie, you've become the best version of yourself and I'm here for it. Julie, you have the courage of a thousand Haley Joel Osments."

"That name sounds familiar," Libbie said. "Who's that again?"

"The little boy who sees dead people in *The Sixth Sense*," Julie said.

"I thought he was in *Die Hard*," Libbie said.

"No, Bruce Willis is in *Die Hard* and also in *The Sixth Sense*," Julie said. "Greg would die a second time if he heard you say that."

"And you?" Kate prompted. "What compliment does Rebecca have for herself?"

"I'm a good companion to all my four-legged friends," Rebecca said.

"Better than good," Kate said. "You're incredible."

Libbie glanced at her phone. "Ethan left the package at the door. I'll be right back."

"How do you know?" Rebecca asked.

"He texted me. I told him not to knock or it would set off

the dogs." Libbie hurried to the door and returned to the kitchen a moment later with a sealed plastic bag filled with herbs.

"Our lawyer is our herb dealer," Kate said, nodding her approval.

"Technically, I'm the herb dealer," Libbie said. "He's my handler." She opened the bag and handed it to Rebecca. "Here you go."

"One of us," Julie began to chant, and Libbie and Kate quickly joined in.

Rebecca stared blankly at the contents of the bag. "I don't know what to do with this. If you handed me a bag of crushed Oreos, that would be a different story." Rebecca could whip up a magical milkshake like nobody's business.

"Follow the instructions," Libbie prodded. "You can do it."

Rebecca's inner critic told her that she most certainly could not, but Rebecca forced herself to study the recipe. She didn't want to be left out a day longer than necessary.

"I would chop it a little finer," Libbie said, observing Rebecca as she worked the blade of the knife over the herbs. She lacked Libbie's finesse, but she got the job done in the end.

"What's the base?" Kate asked.

"Gin," Rebecca said, removing the bottle from the cabinet. She measured the right amount and dumped it into a squat glass. Then she added the herbal mixture and stirred. "This is going to be like drinking orange juice with pulp." She stared at the cocktail with a curled lip. "I hate pulp."

"I love pulp," Libbie said.

"Then you can drink it." Rebecca thrust the glass toward her friend.

"Afraid this one is all you," Libbie told her.

"Come on," Kate urged, "you've been looking forward to this ever since Libbie made the very first cocktail."

Kate was right, yet Rebecca felt a sense of foreboding that made her uncomfortable. Why was she so apprehensive now? She shook it off and raised the glass to her lips.

The other women raised their glasses and toasted Rebecca's inclusion. "Down the hatch, witch," Kate declared.

Rebecca inhaled the aroma. If it tasted as good as it smelled, she was happy even if nothing happened afterward. She'd always been satisfied that her friends had found contentment and self-acceptance. She would be fine without. She'd made it this far and there was no reason to think she wouldn't make it another forty years in the same skin.

She took a sip of the cocktail and pressed her lips together, letting the blend of sweet and sour melt on her tongue. "Delicious."

"Come on," Kate urged. "You can't drink it like you're gargling salt water for a sore throat. Pour that down your gullet and get on with it."

Rebecca did as instructed and gulped the cocktail.

"Feel anything?" Libbie prodded.

"I do." Rebecca burped. "Now I don't."

Kate scrunched her nose. "You're worse than my kids."

Angelica leaped onto the island to greet the visitors and four hands reached out at the same time to pet her.

"I have you all trained now," Rebecca teased.

"I don't think you're the one who has us trained," Julie said, angling her head toward the cat.

"Fair point," Rebecca agreed.

Libbie commandeered the blender to experiment with a new recipe, but Rebecca opted not to drink anything else. Her special cocktail was enough for one night and she didn't want to ingest anything that might dilute the effects. She also wanted to keep a clear head in case the Doberman needed her in the night. She made sure to check on him periodically. The other dogs had sniffed at the bedroom door earlier, aware that another animal had joined their ranks, but they'd seen enough animals come and go that they weren't overly concerned.

"You'll tell us if anything happens, won't you?" Kate asked, once they were ready to depart.

"You know I will."

That night Rebecca slept in the guest bedroom to keep a watchful eye on the Doberman. He didn't seem to mind the company. Only Angelica complained and scratched at the door because she was accustomed to sleeping directly next to Rebecca. The other animals happily piled onto Rebecca's bed whether she was in it or not.

As she tried to sleep, fear and worry returned to gnaw at her insides. Yes, she'd rescued the Doberman from a horrible existence, but what if the shelter closed and she was forced to relocate all the animals? What if she couldn't find a suitable alternative? She'd taken the dog from the frying pan only to toss him into the fire. Rebecca shifted onto her back and stared at the shadows on the ceiling.

Whatever her gift was, she didn't deserve it.

# CHAPTER FOUR

Rebecca sat in the White Room at the shelter with the Doberman, awaiting Dr. Nate's arrival. She'd scanned the dog for a microchip just to confirm he hadn't been taken from someone else. She heard the sound of the main door opening and closing. Charlotte Bernstein was already in the courtyard with the small dogs. Charlotte's husband and three children also volunteered at the shelter during different shifts, but she wasn't expecting them until the weekend.

Peaches poked her head in the doorway and smiled. "Hey."

"Hey, I wasn't expecting you now."

"I know, but I let Nova take my shift at work instead. She needs a new dishwasher." Peaches eyed the Doberman. "Who's this beautiful guy?"

"No name yet." Rebecca stroked the dog's back.

"Any idea how old he is?"

"The man I rescued him from said maybe three, but I'm not so sure."

Peaches smiled. "I don't know. He could be a hundred and

still look like a young dog. He has one of those faces, you know?"

Rebecca smiled and looked at the dog. "You're right. Why don't we call him Paul Rudd?"

Peaches frowned. "Who's that?"

Rebecca looked at her askance. "I'm going to pretend you didn't say that." She leaned her face closer to the dog. "How would you feel about that, Paul Rudd? You're both beautiful, ageless males."

"I'll take your word for it," Peaches said.

"It's called Google. You should try it sometime." Her phone pinged with a text from Dr. Nate, telling her he'd be there shortly. "Looks like your health check will have to wait a bit longer, Paul Rudd."

Peaches observed her carefully. "You seem different today."

Rebecca shrank back. "Do I?" She wasn't about to tell Peaches about the magical cocktail, especially since nothing seemed to have happened. Leave it to Rebecca to get a recipe that turned out to be a lemon.

Peaches slipped off her backpack and unzipped the front compartment. "I'm going to read your cards."

Rebecca waved her off. "Dr. Nate will be here soon."

"You said he's running late, so there's time." She shuffled a pack of tarot cards and fanned them out on the metal table by the door. "Choose three."

Rebecca walked over and quickly chose three.

"Very decisive," Peaches said. "I like it." She flipped over the cards and studied their faces. "Okay."

"Okay? Is that good or bad?" She saw the images of a man with swords sticking out of his back, a burning tower, and a sun.

Peaches tapped the first card. "This Ten of Swords card is

no bueno, but the good news is it's in the past position, so whatever the unwelcome surprise or bad thing is, it's already happened."

Rebecca swallowed hard. No doubt that unwelcome surprise was named Brian Shea.

"The middle card doesn't look great either," Rebecca said. People were jumping out of a burning building. No way could that be good.

"That's called The Tower and it's in the present position."

"And?" Rebecca prompted.

"Crisis. Destruction. Sudden change."

Well, that fit. "And what about the last card?"

"The Sun in the future position means everything's going to work out in your favor."

That was a relief. "Does it say when?"

Peaches laughed. "It's not a schedule. It's your potential future."

She contemplated the unpleasant card. "How long will my present last?"

Peaches scooped up the cards and placed them back in the packet. "Who can say?"

Rebecca wished someone could because that card looked terrifying.

Peaches seemed to notice her anxious expression. "The Sun is here to remind you that good days are ahead of you."

Rebecca saw no sign of the sun today. Not outside and certainly not internally. "Thanks, Peaches."

The young woman patted Rebecca's arm. "You're a bright light for everyone and everything around you. You only need to find that light within yourself to be complete."

Her assessment reminded Rebecca of Libbie's compliment that referred to her as a lighthouse in a storm. Too bad Rebecca viewed herself as nothing more than a dinghy with a hole in the middle.

She managed a smile. "Everyone's a work in progress." Peaches was too young to recognize this. It was, Rebecca had discovered, a lesson to be learned—the hard way.

"What's on the inventory list?" Peaches asked. "I can make a run to the store while I'm here."

"Could you? That would be great. Wet food for dogs and cats, liquid laundry detergent, dry dog food—make sure it's the chicken flavor."

Peaches made a note on her phone. "And I'll add a vanilla latte and a breakfast burrito to that list."

Rebecca straightened. "What makes you think I didn't eat?"

Peaches fixed her with a penetrating gaze. "Did you?"

Rebecca glanced away. "I had…air."

"Exactly. I shall return with sustenance for all," Peaches proclaimed to the masses. A few of the dogs howled in response.

A sense of gratitude washed over Rebecca. "You're a superstar."

"You can't help anybody if you don't fuel your own tank." Peaches tucked away her phone. "See you in an hour, boss."

Charlotte returned from the courtyard and Rebecca asked her to sit with Paul Rudd so she could return to the reception room and await Dr. Nate.

The buzzer sounded and Rebecca came out from behind the counter to open the door for their visitor. An elderly man stood outside with a cat carrier at his feet.

"Mr. Barton, you're right on time." She crouched down to say hello to the orange tabby cat. "How's our friend today?"

"Not looking forward to being neutered, I can tell you that much."

Rebecca's knees cracked as she resumed a standing position. "Come on in. Dr. Nate is running a few minutes behind schedule, but he called to say he'll be here soon."

She took the handle of the carrier, knowing he must have struggled to lift it as far as he did. Mr. Barton was in his early eighties and the recipient of one of the shelter's subsidies for an animal companion. He couldn't afford to pay for the full cost of the surgery, so Cloverleaf Critters would pay the difference. It also helped that Dr. Nate offered a reduced fee for his services.

She set the carrier on the counter and whispered to the cat to help him feel more at ease. "How are things going with Theo?"

"No good," Iago squawked.

Rebecca ignored the parrot.

"Terrific," Mr. Barton said. "He likes to sleep on my pillow. Makes it nice and warm for me at bedtime, although I could do without the cat hair. Tickles my nose."

Rebecca laughed. "One of the downsides, for sure."

The door opened and Rebecca glanced over his shoulder, expecting to see Dr. Nate. Instead, Brian Shea walked through the doorway, followed by a man and a woman she didn't recognize.

"Mr. Shea, I wasn't expecting to see you today," she said.

On cue, the dogs in the main room immediately started barking. They really had a sixth sense about this guy.

"This is Mr. Coates of Coates Enterprises, and his realtor, Miss Hernandez. We'll be touring the building for the next thirty minutes or so."

Rebecca stared at him, her anger rising. "Now isn't convenient for us," she said in a clipped tone.

The prospective buyer glanced uneasily at his companions. "We can come back later. My apologies. I assumed we'd cleared the time with you."

Rebecca's body tensed. "I'm afraid no one gave us notice." There was no reason to lie for Brian Shea. She loathed the man.

"I don't see what difference it makes," Brian said. "We're here now. We might as well get on with it."

Rebecca splayed her hands on the counter. "I have a veterinarian coming any minute to perform surgery on this cat, as well as to provide a health check on a recent rescue. I can't have anyone disturbing them."

Brian shot a quick look at the carrier. "What kind of surgery?"

Rebecca met his gaze. "He's being neutered today." She watched the discomfort flicker across his features. Most men responded that way to the word neuter. She almost wanted to say it again for the pleasure of watching him squirm.

"Why don't we come back?" Mr. Coates said. "I don't mind grabbing a coffee first."

Brian glared in her direction. "Nonsense. Your time is valuable and I know you won't be able to make it back up here this week." He stormed ahead, setting off more of the dogs. Miss Hernandez and Mr. Coates reluctantly followed, with Mr. Coates mouthing an apology as he passed by.

Once they were out of earshot, Mr. Barton turned to look at her. "He's a ray of sunshine, isn't he?"

"The bane of my existence at the moment," she admitted. She'd have to tell the volunteers what was going on now. No choice.

"What an ass," Iago squawked.

Mr. Barton grinned. "I like this bird."

As much as Rebecca wanted to eavesdrop on their conversation during the tour, she knew she couldn't follow them without drawing attention to herself. Besides, Dr. Nate would be here any second and Theo's surgery was her priority.

"What's he doing? Forcing you out?" Mr. Barton asked.

"He's selling the building. He gave me notice, but I'm not

sure all the time in the world is enough to find another place as suitable as this one."

"Have you thought about fighting it?"

She shrugged. "He owns the building. If he wants to sell, I can't stop him."

"Are you sure about that? Have you checked the lease agreement? I was a realtor in a past life. There might be a clause that can help you."

She was embarrassed to admit that she hadn't reviewed any paperwork. She'd taken Brian Shea's word at face value. "I'll take a look. Thanks for the advice."

"I wish I could help, but it's been a long time since I've had an active license."

Rebecca offered a rueful smile. "I appreciate the thought."

As soon as Dr. Nate arrived and took over the White Room, she went to the filing cabinet to search for the lease agreement. Ida had signed it last summer so Rebecca hadn't reviewed it personally. Maybe Mr. Barton was right. Maybe there was language in the agreement that she could use to prevent the sale or at least delay it. She clung to the image of the sun on the tarot card. Brighter days were ahead; they had to be. If that burning tower was any indication, it was always darkest before the dawn.

Rebecca climbed onto the treadmill at the gym and hit the buttons to add her age and weight to her selections. She needed to take her frustrations out on gym equipment. After reviewing the entire lease at the shelter, she'd found nothing helpful and finally called a realtor that Julie had mentioned in passing. The realtor had impressed Julie during a visit to her house not long after the death of Julie's mother. Rebecca hoped this MaryAnn Bigglesworth was a miracle worker because she sure needed one right now.

Rebecca plugged in her headphones and chose the 80s music station. There was something about Def Leppard and Bon Jovi that got her legs moving faster. She could still remember being a teenager dancing around her house with a spatula in place of a guitar to shred. Some of her friends had been into moody bands like The Cure and The Smiths, but Rebecca had found their music too maudlin. She didn't need another reason to feel down. She did that enough without external help.

She perked up when she heard the familiar sound of *Living on a Prayer.* During her college years, one of the preppy guys had nicknamed her Jersey because of her love of Bon Jovi. She embraced the nickname with pride.

As the treadmill incline increased, Rebecca overheard the woman on the neighboring treadmill say, "I told him to defrost the chicken this morning. Why is he texting me about it now? How hard is it to remember to defrost a chicken?"

It occurred to Rebecca that the woman was speaking pretty loudly in order for Rebecca to hear with headphones on. She cut a sideways glance at the woman.

"One of these days I'm going to go on strike and then he'll regret it," the woman said.

Rebecca frowned. Was it her imagination or were the woman's lips not moving? When the woman caught her looking, Rebecca offered an awkward smile. The woman quickly averted her gaze. Was she embarrassed to have been overheard? Maybe she noticed Rebecca's headphones and figured she wouldn't be able to hear her.

Rebecca returned her focus to the music and continued her workout. After thirty minutes, she hurried to the locker room to shower. She would've preferred to shower in the comfort of her own bathroom because she didn't like undressing in front of anyone, but she'd already scheduled a lunch date with Tony and had no choice but to wash off the stink. In addition to chin hairs, a thicker trunk, and joint pain, middle age seemed to bring an increase in body odor. She felt fourteen all over again, embarrassed by her own body. Then again, had there ever been a time when she didn't feel embarrassed by it? Even when she was at her physical peak, she didn't recognize it. She would wear a long T-shirt over her bathing suit to hide her slender frame. Her father had been a strict Catholic who would balk at the sight of a bra strap peeking through the fabric of her shirt. Rebecca was always acutely aware of the position of her bra straps. It was so ingrained in her that, even as an adult, she steered clear of anything that would provide a glimpse of her undergarments.

As she opened the door to her locker, she overheard a woman berating herself. "I'm obviously not working out hard enough. I've only lost five pounds in the last two months. I have to be doing something wrong."

Rebecca glanced at her. "Not necessarily. It could be your metabolism. I read an article about how hormones affect our ability to lose weight once women hit a certain age. I know I definitely can't eat the way I used to without consequences."

When she was younger, Rebecca could easily scarf down thousand-calorie meals without a second thought. Although she was still petite, she'd noticed a thickening around the middle that she imagined would only increase with age.

The woman recoiled slightly. "Excuse me?" She seemed annoyed that Rebecca had commented.

"Nothing," she mumbled. "Forget it." She grabbed her bag from her locker and slung the strap over her shoulder.

"I look so fat in these shorts," another woman said. "Why did I think these were okay to wear?"

Rebecca looked at her. "I think you look great. You have an hourglass figure."

The woman looked at her blankly. "Thank you."

Rebecca noticed the volume in the room increase. All the women in the locker room seemed to be talking at once. It was like a high school classroom before the bell rang.

Her head started to throb. What was happening?

For a fleeting moment, she wondered whether she had inherited the same gift as Julie and ghosts were trying to communicate with her, but no. Rebecca realized with horror she was being inundated with the thoughts of everyone around her.

She staggered back and dropped onto the bench. Closing her eyes, she tried to block the noise but to no avail. She tried to focus on one voice at a time to ease the chaos in her mind.

*My butt is too big.*

*I hate my chunky thighs. I'm definitely saving up for liposuction.*

*Why did I burn those muffins? I'm a terrible cook.*

Rebecca grabbed her bag and fled the locker room to get away from the competing sounds. As she raced to the car, her heart was beating so hard, it actually hurt her chest. She slammed the door to the car and kept the windows closed. Only when the voices subsided did she begin to breathe normally again.

How could she possibly show up for a date now? She was unhinged. She glanced at an incoming text. Crap. Tony was already at the restaurant. It was too late to cancel.

Rebecca collected herself and started the car. Okay, so telepathy was her gift. If Julie could handle ghosts, she could handle overhearing other people's thoughts, right?

As she drove to the restaurant, she was struck by the negativity in each thought she'd overheard. All of these women were being so hard on themselves. Part of her wanted to run back to the locker room and tell them how awesome they were. No wonder they'd looked at her strangely. She'd listened to thoughts they had no intention of sharing.

Well, Rebecca wanted a gift—and now she had one.

"Be careful what you wish for," she muttered.

# CHAPTER FIVE

Rebecca had gotten into the habit of meeting for lunch on a first date. Some women she knew preferred to meet for a drink and no meal, but Rebecca liked to see them in the harsh light of day without the haze of dim lighting and alcohol. Evening added a layer of mystique she didn't want. She also liked to observe how her date treated staff. A bartender was one thing, but a server during the busy lunch rush was quite another. Rebecca could tell a lot about a person from the way they treated animals and restaurant staff.

She parked the car and double-checked her makeup in the rearview mirror. Her lipstick was slightly smudged so she reapplied a coat. With her dark waves and olive skin, she could get away with darker shades of lipstick that her friends couldn't.

Her gaze drifted to the restaurant and she found herself hesitating. What if she overheard every internal monologue in the restaurant? Would her head explode?

Her phone pinged with a text from Tony. *Are you here?*

Rebecca drew a deep breath. She could do this. It was only lunch and she was starving anyway.

She hustled into the restaurant. Outdoor dining was one of Rebecca's favorite things in the world. Now that it was spring again, restaurants had opened their outside seating areas.

She was relieved when she recognized Tony from his photos, hovering by the hostess stand. He stood at about five-foot-nine, with light brown hair and a sharp nose. He wore khakis and a collared shirt with loafers. A little on the preppy side for Rebecca, but clothes didn't make the man. Besides, at least he matched his photos. Rebecca couldn't even count the number of times she met a man who must've used decades-old photos of himself online when he had more hair and fewer pounds. Without fail, those were also the men who expected to date younger, more attractive women.

"Tony?"

He broke into a broad smile when he spotted her. "Rebecca," he said.

They endured an awkward moment where she thrust out a hand to shake his and he leaned down to kiss her cheek, so she ended up stabbing him in the chest with her fingernails. Not the best start to a date.

She laughed. "I'm glad we finally got to meet in person." They'd been talking online for about three weeks, but nothing substantive. She looked forward to getting to know him better.

The hostess picked up two menus from her stand. "Outside or inside today, folks?"

They answered in unison. Unfortunately they gave opposite answers.

"You don't want to sit outside on a beautiful day?" Rebecca asked.

"I hate when gnats end up in my drink," he said with a shrug.

"There's no humidity," Rebecca countered. "It's only May."

Gnats didn't become an issue until later in summer. Still, she didn't want to argue and make a bad impression.

The hostess looked from one to the other. "So, inside then?"

Rebecca forced a smile. "Yes, inside is great. Thank you."

They followed the hostess to a table and Rebecca was grateful to be seated by the window that faced the lake. Small consolation. She glanced longingly at the view. Well, she wasn't here for the sun. She was here for the date with Tony.

They sat across from each other and Rebecca was vaguely annoyed when he switched chairs to the one adjacent to her. It was a personal space issue for her, but she didn't feel comfortable making a fuss. It wasn't as though he tried to sit on her lap. If he did, she wouldn't hesitate to stick the fork in his butt.

"You're much prettier in person," he said.

"Thank you." Rebecca didn't disagree. She hated the way she looked in photographs. "I was pleased to see that you resemble yours as well."

He chuckled. "You wouldn't believe some of the women I've dated. I think at least one of them used her engagement photo from her first marriage and cut out the husband. You could still see part of his arm."

She'd seen similar profiles where the man is clearly wearing the tuxedo from his own wedding. People made strange choices sometimes.

They studied their respective menus. "What are your thoughts on seafood?" she asked.

"Can't get enough of it. You?"

"Never met a creature from the deep I didn't want to eat." She paused. "Okay, that sounds horrible. I'd never eat a whale or a dolphin."

"How about a shark?" he asked, his eyes twinkling with mischief.

She contemplated the idea of a sharkburger. It had potential. "With the right side dishes, I think it could work."

He chuckled and Rebecca realized she didn't mind his adjacent chair anymore. It created an air of intimacy that she was currently enjoying.

The server took their order and she noted his impeccable manners. So he disliked gnats in his drink. Who didn't?

They chatted in earnest about their food preferences. Rebecca grew so relaxed that she forgot all about the telepathy she'd experienced in the gym. Maybe it had been a fluke.

She and Tony bonded over a shared love of gnocchi and found common ground in entertainment. They both had a soft spot for *The Goonies*, although they disagreed on whether Keanu Reeves or Paul Rudd was more ageless. She'd mentioned Paul Rudd at the shelter and he'd countered with Keanu.

Rebecca thought the date was going well, certainly much better than the last date she'd been on when the man had talked of nothing but himself and failed to ask her a single question. She actually made a game of seeing how long he could go without asking her anything about herself. Turned out it was the entire date. She was shocked at the end of the lunch when he'd asked to see her again. When she turned him down, he'd expressed surprise, saying what a good time they'd had. Rebecca had been nothing more than an object for him to talk at and boast about his Audi and his accelerated retirement plan. Naturally he'd enjoyed himself and wanted to do it again.

The food arrived and Rebecca resisted the urge to devour the plate whole. Now that she'd decided she liked him, she wanted to be on her best behavior.

"Have you ever been married?" she asked. Most of the men she met had an ex-wife, and she was always curious to see how they spoke about her. If vitriol and blame spilled from his lips, she would know he wasn't a keeper. Of course, with her new skill, she'd probably be able to hear what he thought about her even if he didn't say it.

As if on cue, she heard his voice in her head—*Ugh. I hate this part.*

Now Rebecca was curious. What did he hate? The idle conversation or talking about his ex-wife?

"I've been married twice, actually," he said.

Ah. No wonder he didn't like this part. She was surprised it hadn't come up in their online exchanges. "Both divorces?"

"Yeah. Both more expensive than the weddings too." His smile indicated that he was joking.

"Any kids?"

"One with each," he said. "Amy lives in Villanova and Melanie lives in Doylestown."

She cocked her head. "And now you're here? That must be tough, being apart from your kids."

"This is my second home," he said. "My primary residence is in Conshohocken, so it's roughly between the two kids."

Okay, that wasn't so terrible.

"How often are you up here?" she asked. It would be difficult to have a meaningful relationship with someone who was bouncing between two kids and a primary house elsewhere, although if she liked him enough, she'd make it work.

"I work from home, so that gives me flexibility with location. I try to get up here when the weather's good. I love to fish. And I'm bringing both kids here this summer. They love the lake." *That reminds me. I need to call the nanny back about her requested vacation days.* "This food is amazing, by the way. Do you want to try some?"

"Sure." Rebecca was pleasantly surprised when he fed her from his own fork. It was a sensual moment, gazing into his eyes as she took his fork in her mouth and swallowed. She initially thought he might be boring, but Tony was turning out to be more promising than she expected.

She finished her lunch and wondered whether they'd continue to linger. The shelter had coverage and she wasn't due at the library until seven.

"What are your thoughts on dessert?" he asked. *I've got my eye on that key lime pie.*

Her spirits lifted. She loved key lime pie too. "Dessert is always a yes for me."

"Perfect. What will you have?"

"Key lime pie," she said.

He smiled. "I love that we have so much in common."

Rebecca agreed. "If you'll excuse me, I just need the restroom." Unfortunately her bladder seemed to shrink with each passing year of her life.

Once in the restroom, she took the opportunity to check in with the shelter and make sure everything was okay. She also noticed a missed call from MaryAnn, the realtor. Crap. She needed to schedule viewings.

Their server emerged from the stall and washed her hands at the sink. "How's your date going? First one, right?"

"It is," she said. "How did you know?"

The server smiled. "I see a lot of first dates, although not too many during the lunch hour. You two seem to be hitting it off."

Rebecca's cheeks grew flushed. "Thanks. I think so too."

She practically skipped back to the table, eager to continue their conversation and enjoy a slice of heaven. As she threaded her way through the other tables, her gaze met his and he smiled.

*Dessert will be quick, maybe another fifteen minutes tops. The food was great, so lunch wasn't a complete waste of time. I'd definitely come back to this place, just not with her.*

By the time she returned to her seat, Rebecca's rising

spirits had deflated. She had no idea the date wasn't going well for him. He seemed to be enjoying himself as much as she was. She tried not to let her disappointment show as she slid back into her seat. She chose to focus on the pie in front of her. Like he said, not a complete waste of time.

"This place is great. Thanks for recommending it."

"No problem," she said.

Great. Now she was sure to run into him in the future on other dates when he was on other dates. She'd make sure to always choose an outdoor table, which is what she preferred anyway. At least he didn't live here full-time.

Rebecca finished her pie in silence as he continued to chatter, oblivious to her sour mood. With an encouraging wink at Rebecca, the server swooped past the table and dropped the bill.

*I bet she doesn't even try to pay*, Tony thought. *Someone who runs a shelter probably expects a handout.*

Rebecca balked. She'd taken care of herself for her entire adult life and never expected a man to pay.

She snapped open her purse and removed her wallet. "I've got this," she said, dazzling him with a smile. "This place was my suggestion, so I'll pay."

His face registered surprise. "If you insist. This was fun. We should do it again sometime."

And by sometime, Rebecca knew he meant never. Why bother saying that when he didn't mean it? If she hadn't been able to read his mind, she would be waiting around wondering when he would call. Possibly even putting off other dates to make room for him. It served no one to lie.

She kept her smile intact. "You know what? I don't see this working out," she said. "I'm really looking for someone who's here full-time."

Rebecca paid quickly so she could make her escape.

"Well, if that's how you feel…" he said. "It was a pleasure meeting you."

Part of her wanted to know more. What was so off-putting about her that he didn't want a second date? He didn't seem to have any specific thoughts as to his reasons and there'd been nothing that happened during the date to signal a problem.

"Good luck finding wife number three," she said. She slid her arm through the loop of her purse handle and vacated the chair.

*Well, that was an unexpected development*, he mused.

Rebecca turned on her heel and hurried from the restaurant before her emotions made a fool of her. By the time she got into her car, she could no longer contain the tears. They slid down her cheeks in fat drops and she smudged her foundation in her effort to wipe them away. She wasn't really sure why she was crying. She didn't like him *that* much. It was the fact that he'd rejected her without rhyme or reason that bothered her the most. They'd enjoyed themselves. He seemed to like her appearance. They had common ground.

Rebecca exhaled loudly. None of it mattered. She still hadn't been good enough.

She tucked away the tissue and started the car. She would return to her safe space where she knew she was always wanted. They didn't call it a shelter for nothing.

## CHAPTER SIX

"It was that bad, huh?" Libbie asked.

Rebecca sat at the table in Libbie's kitchen, giving her friend the rundown of her newfound ability and its role during the awful date. She'd tried seeking solace at the shelter, but the intrusive thoughts of the volunteers caused a headache to bloom. Normally Rebecca enjoyed listening to their chitchat. Combined with the inner monologues, though, the noise became too much for her and she escaped to Libbie's house for peace and quiet, as well as a bit of emotional support.

"I think your gift is interesting." Libbie remained at the counter as she worked on a new recipe for garlic knots. Any other time Rebecca would be anxiously awaiting the finished product, but she was too full from lunch to care. Her scale would thank her later.

"It isn't consistent. I seemed to hear everyone at the gym, then only Tony at the restaurant."

"And then everyone at the shelter," Libbie finished for her. "Can you hear mine now?"

Rebecca shook her head. "I think I'm too distracted by the

pain to hear anything." She leaned her elbows on the table and pressed her hands against her cheeks. "This is the worst gift ever. Where's my receipt? I'll even spring for return shipping."

Libbie cast her a sympathetic glance. "I'm not surprised you feel like garbage. It's a lot to take on all of the sudden."

Rebecca still hadn't told her friends about the shelter situation. She didn't want to add another woeful tale to their conversation. As it was, she felt like a source of never-ending negativity.

"What does your book tell you?" Libbie asked.

Rebecca frowned at her. "What book?"

Libbie rolled another ball of dough. "Your recipe book from Inga."

Rebecca recovered from her slouched position. "You think the book might have another recipe?"

Libbie snorted. "Have you not been paying attention? None of our books stopped at the first cocktail recipe. By the time we're old, those books will read like a story."

A story told by recipes. Rebecca liked that idea. "Mine's in the car. Let me grab it."

Libbie shot her a quizzical look. "Why do you keep it in the car?"

"I don't usually. I have my adoption program at the library later and I'd been planning to do a little research while I was there."

Libbie slid a baking tray into the oven and turned to face her. "What kind of research?" She set the timer for twenty minutes and wiped her hands on her apron.

"It was before the telepathy started at the gym. I was going to look up everything in the recipe and see if I could figure out what my gift would be." She rubbed her temples. "Except now I know."

"You thought you'd figure it out at the library?" Libbie scoffed. "You'd be better off talking to Lorraine."

"She was on my list too," Rebecca said.

Libbie washed her hands at the kitchen sink. "Well, now you know. Problem solved."

"I don't know about that. I'd say the problem's just beginning." After all her complaining about being the last one to get a recipe and now she was complaining about the gift she received. Rebecca could hardly stand her own company at the moment.

"What's wrong with being telepathic?" Libbie returned to her bowl of dough and started on another batch.

"It's horrible, Lib. I don't want to know what people are thinking."

Libbie gave her a pointed look. "You don't want to know what they're thinking in general or what they're thinking about you?"

"Can it be both?" The women at the gym weren't thinking about her specifically, but being privy to their thoughts still made her uncomfortable.

Libbie kept her focus on the knots. "Look, I'm not going to pretend to be the expert here, but maybe think about what the universe is trying to teach you. If there's one thing we've learned since this whole thing started, you weren't randomly given the power of telepathy. There's a reason this is the gift you, Rebecca Angelos, were given. If you can figure out why that is, you'll be that much closer to embracing it."

Rebecca managed a small smile. "See? This is why I came to you. I feel better already." She hoped Libbie was right, although she couldn't imagine what lesson involved eavesdropping on other people's private thoughts. "Let me grab the recipe book from my car. We can brainstorm together."

Hercules lifted his head when Rebecca vacated her chair and she could tell the dog was debating whether to follow. If there was the chance for a walk outside, Hercules was all over it.

"Not now," Libbie said, anticipating the dog's next move.

Rebecca laughed as she hurried outside to the car and retrieved the book from under the passenger seat where she'd safely stored it. She tucked it under her arm and returned to the house to find Hercules waiting by the door.

"Sorry, boy," she said and patted his head. The dog lowered his head in disappointment, prompting a laugh from Libbie.

"Come on, Mr. Persistent," she said, opening the back door. "Knock yourself out."

The dog bolted through the doorway as Rebecca opened the book on the counter. "Do you think we might learn more by looking at the recipe?"

As a chef and the first recipient of a cocktail recipe, Libbie's herbal knowledge far surpassed Rebecca's so she was more than willing to listen to her friend's insights. Libbie even had an impressive garden in the backyard filled with ingredients that she used to help the people of Lake Cloverleaf.

"Give me one second to finish this tray." Libbie rolled the final ball of dough and placed it on the tray. "This was Courtney's request. She wanted me to try adding cheese to the garlic knots. Not exactly a culinary masterpiece, but it will appease the masses."

Rebecca inhaled the scent of garlic in the air. "It smells amazing." Then again, Rebecca loved the smell of garlic in a kitchen. It reminded her of Sundays with her parents. They'd go to church in the mornings and then her mom would make a big Sunday dinner that usually involved a generous amount of garlic.

Libbie joined her at the end of the counter and flipped to the next page of the book. "What's this one?"

Rebecca glanced down at the page to see an unfamiliar recipe. "A second one?" Had it been there before and she'd missed it?

Libbie laughed. "I told you. The universe definitely seems to know what you need right now."

Sure enough, upon closer inspection, Rebecca saw that the recipe was designed to treat a psychic hangover. "How do you treat a hangover with a cocktail?"

Libbie tapped the bottom of the page. "Says here you can substitute tea for alcohol." She smiled. "Want to try it? I think I have everything we need."

"I would love you forever if this works." Rebecca had taken painkillers at the shelter, but they hadn't touched her headache. She was rapidly reaching the point where she wanted to curl into a ball and swaddle herself in darkness. She couldn't afford to be incapacitated right now, not with everything going on.

Libbie scanned the list of ingredients. "Come out to the garden and I'll show you what we need." She swiped an empty glass jar off the ledge on her way outside.

Rebecca followed her and realized that another companion had joined their quest. Eliza, the cat Libbie had inherited from Inga, stood at the edge of the garden. Rebecca watched the cat's tail flick back and forth as she surveyed the rows of plants.

"I feel like she has an opinion," Libbie said, sounding amused.

"I bet she does," Rebecca said. "Animals are more in tune to nature than we are most of the time."

"Maybe so, but I don't think they're in tune to recipes or I'd enlist both of mine to join my staff."

Sensing he was a topic of discussion, Hercules dropped the stick from his mouth and ran over to them.

"Being busy is a good problem to have," Rebecca reminded her.

"Don't I know it. Every time I pay a bill from my own bank account and have money left over, I'm grateful." Libbie handed the jar to Rebecca. "We need mint and lavender."

Rebecca could identify those two easily enough. "Anything else?"

"Chamomile."

Rebecca drank chamomile tea all the time, but she didn't know how to identify it in the garden. "Any hints?"

Libbie laughed as Eliza sprinted across the garden to a bed of flowers that reminded Rebecca of daisies. "Someone really wants to help."

Rebecca's brow lifted. "They're chamomile?"

Eliza investigated the flowers and was momentarily distracted by a passing butterfly.

"They are," Libbie confirmed. "I guess the cat's been paying more attention than I thought."

"I've been missing out. I need to train Angelica to gather the ingredients for my meals," Rebecca joked. She could only imagine what the cat would choose to make. Anchovy and tuna on liver crackers, most likely. "What else do we need?"

"Rose hips, but they're over there." Libbie pointed to the back end of the yard where Rebecca spotted a cluster of small red berries.

"Those are rose hips?"

"Yep. I don't prune back my roses as much as I should solely for this purpose. Rose hips are great to have on hand."

Rebecca removed a few and dropped them into the jar with the mint and lavender. "What else?"

"You need enough for a tablespoon."

Rebecca plucked a few more rose hips and added them to the jar. She turned toward Libbie expectantly.

"Everything else is inside. I have fresh honey from Bernie

the Beekeeper." Libbie started toward the house and Rebecca followed with the jar.

"Do you think his name is really Bernie or he changed it for the sake of alliteration?" Not that she blamed him. Rebecca was a sucker for alliteration.

Libbie laughed. "Come on. Let's make a witches brew and cure your magic hangover."

Rebecca mixed the ingredients together under Libbie's watchful eye. She knew she wasn't as adept as Libbie in the kitchen, but the kitchen had never been Rebecca's domain. She was perfectly content to eat premade meals and takeout, although she worried that lifestyle would catch up with her body sooner or later. She was lucky to have made it this far without significant weight gain. Her petite frame was purely down to genetics rather than her choices though. Her parents were both on the smaller side, although their bodies had grown much softer than Rebecca's in their retirement years.

Rebecca added boiling water to the mixture and inhaled the pleasant aroma. "I think we did it."

"*You* did it," Libbie said. "I only stood behind you and cheered."

She brought the mug to her mouth and sipped carefully.

"What's the verdict?" Libbie prompted.

"Tastes good." A few more sips and Rebecca's headache melted away. "It's a miracle cure."

"Not exactly. It's designed to help with your specific problem," Libbie said.

"Bah! You and your logic. I prefer a miracle cure." She swallowed another mouthful now that the temperature had cooled. "I guess I'd better keep a batch of this ready."

"Not a bad idea, especially while you adjust to your telepathy. I'm sure it's a lot for your head to handle."

"Not only my head. It's hard to hear people's thoughts

when they're being hard on themselves. I was emotionally invested after two seconds. I wanted to tell all the women in the gym they're goddesses." Telepathy was impacting her mind, body, and spirit.

Libbie rubbed her friend's arm. "You can do this. I know you can."

Rebecca offered a rueful smile. "I sure hope so, because it seems like I don't have much of a choice."

# CHAPTER SEVEN

REBECCA WOLFED down leftover spaghetti and drank two more cups of water to reach her goal of six cups per day. If she didn't use her phone to keep track of how many cups of water she drank, she would forget to drink it altogether. Her doctor had suggested getting a cup with the ounces marked on the side and Rebecca had immediately ordered one online. She was prone to dehydration and tracking the ounces definitely helped.

She made sure to feed the animals and take them outside to stretch their legs before she headed to the library for her session on animal adoption. Sugar and Spice didn't want to leave her side tonight. The corgi mix and the greyhound seemed to sense she had a busy evening ahead and chose that moment to stick to her like glue.

"This is your chance to run amok," she advised them. "Better take advantage of it."

Watching them run—or in Sugar's case waddle—around the yard, a sense of envy crept over her. They were so free to be themselves without judgment. Sugar didn't worry that her corgi butt looked too big. Spice wasn't concerned that he was too thin and that people would suspect he had an eating disorder. Oh, to be a dog. But then her thoughts turned to Paul Rudd and some of the animals in the shelter that had been rescued from unhappy homes. There was no chance they could've helped themselves. They were entirely dependent on people to improve their situations. *That* Rebecca didn't envy.

She ushered the animals back inside and grabbed a cotton sweater to wear over her short-sleeved top. Someone in the library insisted on cranking up the air-conditioning the moment the calendar flipped to May and Rebecca was determined to be prepared this time instead of letting her teeth chatter for an hour.

She looked forward to her talks at the library. They presented an opportunity to provide a community service, not just with information about animal adoption but with connection. There were a few people who showed up every month simply to chat with her and each other. She knew some of them were lonely and that a pet could make a world of difference to them if she could only persuade them to take the leap. Many of them had never cared for a pet before and didn't feel equipped, especially the older ones. One woman in particular stood out to Rebecca. Miriam was eighty-two and her husband had been allergic, so they'd never had a pet. He passed away two years ago and Rebecca knew Miriam was incredibly lonely at home. A dog would probably be too much for her, but a cat would be an ideal companion. For the past few months, Miriam had been showing up to the library to listen to Rebecca's talk, but not willing to take the next step. Maybe tonight would be the night. Simon would be perfect for someone like Miriam. Rebecca even made sure to have updated photos of him on her phone to share. She knew if could get Miriam to come to the shelter that she'd probably walk out with Simon. Rebecca was more than willing to help her set everything up at home. She'd done that for plenty of people. Over the years, she'd learned that certain people needed a bit of handholding, but once they were up and running, they were more than capable.

This evening the library was more active than it usually was at this hour and she wondered if there'd been a meeting or a talk right before hers.

"Nice to see you, Rebecca," the librarian said as Rebecca blew past the counter.

"You too," Rebecca replied in a loud whisper.

She spotted her group clustered by the doorway of the Community Room.

"I'm here," she said. "Make way. Coming through."

"Oh, good," a scratchy voice said. "I was beginning to think you bailed on us."

Rebecca turned and smiled. "You can't get rid of me that easily, Herb."

"Good, because you're my cheap entertainment tonight," he replied. "Nothing good on television except those reality shows and they're not very realistic at all. Did I tell you about the one where they have to live in the woods without clothes or supplies?" He shook his head. "What's realistic about that?"

Rebecca smiled. "I think you might have mentioned that show once or twice." Or every single time she saw him.

They assembled in the room and Rebecca took her place at the front. She was glad to spot Miriam slip in and take the seat next to Herb. Hopefully she could corner her about Simon afterward.

The moment she opened her mouth to speak, she felt a hot flash coming on. Inwardly she groaned. Terrific timing. She shrugged off her sweater.

"Helen, would you mind leaving the door open?" Rebecca asked the white-haired woman.

"Sure thing, honey. Wait until you're my age. You'll be cold all the time. I swear my skin is made of Swiss cheese. The air seems to blow right through me straight to my bones."

Right now Rebecca would gladly trade places with Helen. She was glad she'd given her underarms an extra swipe of deodorant earlier. She hadn't given body odor a second thought since middle school, yet here she was in her late forties and worried about her pungent scent. Nobody warned her about this stage of development in seventh grade health class.

"What's today's topic?" Herb asked. "I even brought my pencil tonight." He twirled his yellow pencil in the air.

*I hope she covers the basics*, a woman thought. *I'm not sure I can do this, but Marc really wants a dog.*

Rebecca glanced to the opposite side of the room where a young couple sat with their chairs pushed together.

"I think I'll discuss the basics of animal care and common behavioral issues for first-time companions." She avoided the term pet owner, believing the relationship was more symbiotic than the term ownership implied.

*Thank goodness*. The woman smiled at her husband. *If I can't find a way to balance our work schedules and a dog, then we shouldn't even consider having children anytime soon.*

Rebecca tried to give a broad overview of the topic and gave references for those who wanted to delve further into a specific topic. Behavioral issues were the hardest to address without examples, which was why she stuck to the most common issues. She made sure to touch on cats as well, if only to prime the pump for her conversation with Miriam afterward.

Toward the end of her spiel, a figure in the doorway drew her attention. Ruggedly handsome, the man appeared to be in his forties with golden brown hair that skimmed his shoulders. She'd been a sucker for men with long hair ever since her Bon Jovi days.

Their eyes locked and she paused to smile at him. "You're more than welcome to join us. There's plenty of room."

He seemed taken aback. "I'm sorry. I didn't mean to interrupt."

"Not at all," Herb said. "The more, the merrier. Come in."

Bless Herb. He'd talk to the lamppost if there was any hope of it talking back.

Bon Jovi slipped into the room and took a seat at the back. She tried to tune in to his thoughts, but everything was operating at a low hum now. Other than the young woman's occasional thoughts, Rebecca heard only white noise. She wasn't sure whether it was the way her gift worked or whether it was the psychic hangover cure taking the edge off.

Once she finished her overview, Rebecca opened the floor for questions. The young woman raised her hand. "My husband and I both work out of the house. Do you think it's selfish for us to adopt a dog?"

Her husband nudged her, seemingly embarrassed by the question.

"I'm not here to judge your choices," Rebecca said, "but the fact that you're even asking that question is a good sign. I think it all depends on the set-up you have. Do you both work long hours or is it more nine-to-five? Do you have a fenced-in yard and a doggy door? Will someone walk the dog during the day when you're not there? Will you crate train?"

"Lots to think about," the young woman said, eyeing her husband. Rebecca could tell she still wasn't sure and that was okay. At least they weren't adopting a cute puppy for Christmas with no preparation. Those people inevitably were the type to surrender the dog later once the dog proved to be a living, breathing creature with a mind of her own rather than an adorable accessory.

Rebecca plucked a business card from her purse and crossed the room to place it in front of the couple. "I'm available for questions anytime. There's no need to rush into a decision. Trust me—there will always be a dog in need of adoption."

"See you next week," Herb called over his shoulder. "The bus is here. Gotta go."

The local bus system was one of the perks of living in Lake Cloverleaf. In the summers, the bus delivered children to camp, and delivered their parents to adult activities. It was, Rebecca had discovered, one of the downsides of not being a mother in town. She would have loved to ride the bus with the other women and taken advantage of some of the adult recreation programs that included fun activities like volleyball or the adventure race. Sometimes Rebecca's inner child screamed for attention, but she wasn't sure how to indulge it without looking out of place. It seemed the only adults who took part in the activities were the ones with kids at camp. Inevitably the conversation would turn to kids and Rebecca hated feeling left out. It was better to not join in the first place. She'd been so relieved when she hit her forties if only because she started making friends whose children were either grown or who didn't have them at all. Meeting Inga had changed her life in more ways than one. It was as though the older woman knew what Rebecca lacked in her life and was determined to provide it for her. Although Libbie and Kate both had children, they also had a sense of self. They never made Rebecca feel isolated or 'other.' It was a gift her friends didn't even realize they possessed. The fact that Julie and Greg didn't have children also helped Rebecca feel less alone.

"Miriam, do you have a minute?"

Miriam stopped her shuffle toward the door and turned to face Rebecca. "I need to catch the bus too, dear. Do you need me for something?"

Rebecca waved her off. "No, it's fine. Next time." Maybe she'd invite Miriam to the shelter as a volunteer. If the older woman grew comfortable around the animals, she might eventually feel confident enough to take one home.

Miriam gave her a thumbs up. "Great talk."

As Rebecca gathered her belongings, she noticed the attractive man lingering at the back of the room. "Is there something I can help you with?"

"Actually, I was wondering if you make house calls," he said.

Rebecca angled her head. "I'm not a veterinarian, you know."

"Oh, I know," he said, thrusting his hands into the pockets of his jeans. "You just seem to know a lot about animal behavior and my sister's been struggling with her dog. I was thinking maybe you'd be a good person to offer her some pointers." He paused. "We'd pay you for your time, of course. I wouldn't expect you to do it for free."

"Has she tried a class? I can recommend one in town."

"She went to one, but the other owners were apprehensive and she felt like they'd be happier if she didn't come back. Her dog is sweet, but extremely energetic and friendly."

She laughed, slinging her bag over her shoulder and heading toward the door. "I can think of worse things to be. What kind of dog does she have?"

"Husky. Or a barking bundle of energy, as we like to say."

Rebecca offered a sympathetic smile. "Here." She produced another business card and handed it to him. "Why don't you have her call me and we'll set something up?"

He glanced at the card. "Rebecca." He stuck out a hand. "Peter Putnam. It's nice to meet you."

Rebecca shook his hand and was immediately struck by the warmth of his skin. Not in a sticky, sweaty way. More... inviting. Her cheeks grew warm and she was glad she hadn't put on her sweater.

"Do you have a dog, Peter?"

"No, I have two cats. AC and DC." *Why did you tell her about the cats already? Women hate when men have cats. They think it's a red flag.*

Rebecca was startled by the sound of his voice in her head. Maybe the fact that they were now alone in the room had reopened her telepathic channel.

"I love their names," she said. "I have cats and dogs. And the occasional goat or ferret. Depends on the week."

He chuckled. "Dare I ask?"

"I'm the director of Cloverleaf Critters. Comes with the territory. I don't think you adopted the cats from my shelter. I would've remembered." She realized her comment sounded either vaguely judgmental or like she was hitting on him. Either way, she suddenly wished she hadn't opened her mouth.

"No, they're Siamese. Adopted them from a woman about thirty minutes from here. My mom used to take in all the neighborhood strays," he explained. "I became a cat person by default. One of the strays was part Siamese. We called him Chip. He only had half a tail."

"Sounds sweet."

"He became my shadow. If I was out in the woods building a fort, Chip was there. If I was in my room with a book, Chip was there on the pillow. I guess I was hoping to create that kind of magical bond with AC and DC."

In forty-seven years, Rebecca had never swooned over a man until now. Well, there'd been plenty of fictional men, but not one standing right in front of her. "Your mom must be pleased that you have carried on her love of cats."

He lowered his gaze. "She died a few years ago. That's when I decided to adopt them. It was a way of keeping part of her spirit with me." *Stop talking now, Peter. You've already said more than you should. What is it about this woman that makes me want to keep talking to her?*

Rebecca grew flustered. She hated that she knew what he was thinking, although admittedly she was thrilled by the contents. She had to get away before she said something stupid and ruined the moment, as she was wont to do.

"It was great to meet you, Peter," she said. "I should get home before the animals stage a revolt."

"Have a good night," he said. "Thanks for the talk."

"No problem." Rebecca left the library with a spring in her step. She wouldn't have described the day as a good one, but things were definitely looking up.

# CHAPTER EIGHT

MaryAnn Bigglesworth was a redhead who dressed for success. Rebecca had noticed her floral dress in the window of a pricey local boutique only two weeks ago. She had no doubt it came with a steep price tag. Still, the realtor wore it well and, if she could afford it, more power to her.

"I've lined up a few properties for us to view today," MaryAnn said, managing that perfect blend of friendly yet professional. "While I've kept your checklist in mind, it wasn't possible to find a building that ticked all the boxes. Then again, real estate is like a marriage. It's all about compromise." *And just like a husband, it's going to take a miracle to find exactly what you're looking for.*

Rebecca smiled. "I'll have to take your word for it. I've never been married."

MaryAnn cringed. "I'm sorry. I shouldn't have assumed. Truth be told, I shouldn't have been married either, but we all make mistakes." Her laugh was surprisingly infectious. Its bubbly nature didn't match her perfectly coiffed exterior.

"Would it help to look around the shelter before we go?" Rebecca offered.

MaryAnn broke into a broad smile. "I was about to request the grand tour." She peered at the parrot. "Who's this gorgeous fellow?"

"His name is Iago and he's very opinionated."

"Pretty girl," the parrot said.

MaryAnn splayed a hand on her chest, flattered. "Why, thank you, kind sir. I could use an ego boost like you at home."

"He saves his insults for me," Rebecca said, knowing perfectly well he was only repeating what she said to herself.

Rebecca took her into the other rooms of the shelter so she could see the layout with the enclosures, including the White Room with its surgical equipment. The dogs were excited to see a newcomer, wagging their tails and barking for attention. MaryAnn didn't seem entirely at ease, but she put on a good show.

*I assume they don't bite. Either way, I'll be sure not to stand too close.*

Next Rebecca showed her the grooming room with its large sinks and shower area for the larger dogs, as well as the outdoor courtyard area. "This works for us, but I'd love a larger space outside if possible."

"Then you'll be pleased to know there are a couple locations on the list today with outdoor space much larger than this." MaryAnn took a final peek in each room on the way back to the front room. "This has been helpful. Thanks."

"Thank *you*. You're going to help these guys avoid homelessness."

MaryAnn painted on a bright smile. "Absolutely." *Dear baby Jesus in a manger, I hope so. I can't be responsible for leaving these animals without a roof over their heads.*

Rebecca felt a pang of guilt. She was putting a lot of pressure on the realtor; it wouldn't be MaryAnn's fault if the right building wasn't available. Brian Shea had given her the proper amount of legal notice, but it would've been better to have longer to prepare for a change of this magnitude. The shelter wasn't a candy store. They required a certain size and infrastructure, as well as outside space.

"I'm happy to drive if that's easier," Rebecca said.

"Absolutely not. Part of my white glove service is providing transport as well." She ushered Rebecca out the door and into her sleek silver Mercedes.

"I might need you to drive me everywhere from now on," Rebecca said, admiring the plush leather interior.

"I'm one of those weird people who loves to drive," MaryAnn admitted.

"I would too if I had a car this nice." Rebecca grew apprehensive as they headed out of the downtown area. "How far how are we going?"

"Only about five more minutes. I think you're going to love this space. There's plenty of land for the animals to enjoy."

Rebecca perked up slightly. "There's a fenced-in yard?"

"No, but there's no busy road nearby and it's on five acres. I figure with your volunteers, there would be plenty of space for long walks or to set up outdoor pens."

Rebecca didn't want to be negative from the outset. She tried to keep an open mind, but already she was feeling like this was a bad choice.

MaryAnn drove along a long gravel driveway to reach the building. It was a single-story brick building with very few windows, which meant limited natural light.

Rebecca tried to imagine what purpose the building had previously served. "What was this place used for?"

"Believe it or not, a local farmer rented his land to a company that sells snowblowers and lawnmowers and tractors. The store itself didn't have enough floor space downtown, so they would keep their overflow here, but they've since relocated the business completely."

MaryAnn parked the car and they entered the dimly lit building. Rebecca didn't think she'd be able to tolerate the lack of natural light and she thought it would be hard on the animals as well. The ceilings were also low, which made the building feel claustrophobic.

*Beggars can't be choosers*, Rebecca reminded herself.

MaryAnn gave a brief overview of the building's stats, but otherwise remained silent, giving Rebecca a chance to look around and form her own opinions.

*Now that I've seen the shelter, I highly doubt she's going to want to lease this place, but with all the space, it's still worth a look. I wouldn't be doing my job if I didn't show it to her.*

Rebecca didn't disagree. The land made a lot of sense, but the building didn't. "I'm afraid this one isn't going to work. The infrastructure isn't here and even if we could make modifications, I don't think there's enough square footage. Our enclosures need to be a minimum of a certain size. Anything smaller is unacceptable."

MaryAnn smiled. "I thought you might say that."

"Where to next?" Rebecca asked as they walked back to the car.

"Meadow Drive. This one has the interior space, but it would also require some modifications."

Rebecca buckled her seatbelt. "I figure everything we look at is going to require adjustments. Our current building developed over time as our needs changed. I highly doubt we're going to find a place that has the infrastructure ready and waiting."

"A pragmatic attitude. I can work with that."

MaryAnn reversed the car and vacated the lot.

Rebecca glanced in the side-view mirror at the retreating

view. She wouldn't have liked being isolated out here either. She worked alone quite a bit. She didn't love the idea of being on her own and neither would the volunteers. The winter months would make the drive to work treacherous too. No thanks.

The next building had larger windows, but the outdoor space was all concrete. The third property was adjacent to a farm, which seemed like a reasonable fit except for the fact that the farmer's chickens roamed freely and he apparently refused to rein them in. That was a disaster waiting to happen as far as Rebecca was concerned. She didn't want to have to return a few remaining feathers to the farmer's doorstep with a note of apology.

By the time they finished viewing their fifth property, Rebecca was more exhausted than she anticipated. What was so tiring about walking around looking at buildings? She had no idea. Clearly she needed more exercise.

"I'm sorry we didn't find the right property today," MaryAnn said. "But if you leave this with me, I'll continue to hunt for you. If there's a viable commercial property for lease in this town, it's not going to escape my notice."

Rebecca gave her a reassuring smile. "I have faith in you. I just don't know that I believe the right property exists. I think I'm kidding myself."

The realtor parked the car in front of the shelter. "You're definitely in a tough spot. I don't envy you there. I think you do remarkable work, though, and it's important to make sure that you're able to continue with it." She paused. "I'm sure I shouldn't say anything because it's unprofessional, but I know Brian Shea. He's not known for his ethics or his kind heart. Full disclosure: at one point I even represented him, but we parted ways two years ago. I won't say what happened. There wasn't anything legally wrong with what he did, but I was uncomfortable with the ethics of it, so I cut ties."

Rebecca had no idea, but the information didn't surprise her. "Thank you for telling me." She was impressed that MaryAnn had the backbone to stand up to someone like Brian Shea and walk away from income.

MaryAnn lowered her voice. "On that note, might I suggest consulting a lawyer?"

"I'm not sure it's worth the effort. I reviewed the lease agreement and he seems to be acting within his rights."

"Even so, a lawyer might be able to find a loophole that prevents you from having to leave. Nothing ventured, nothing gained—that's my motto."

"Thanks, I appreciate the advice." She unbuckled her seatbelt and opened the passenger door. "Let me know when you find something else for us to see. I'll keep my schedule flexible." She didn't have a choice. She knew Brian Shea wouldn't agree to extend the lease. If MaryAnn called, she'd come running.

"If you need the name of a lawyer, I can recommend a few."

Rebecca smiled. "Now that's one task I can handle on my own."


Rebecca first met Ethan Townsend when he revealed the contents of Inga's will. Now he and Libbie were in a serious relationship, which made this clandestine appointment with Ethan mildly uncomfortable for Rebecca. She didn't want to lie to her friends, but she couldn't bear to admit what was happening. Somehow telling her closest friends about the shelter would make the situation real.

"Did you bring the agreement?" Ethan asked.

Rebecca passed it across the desk and into his outstretched hand. "I'm sorry I couldn't email it over sooner. I've been so busy."

"No worries. It's not a lengthy agreement." His eyes remained fixed on the pages as he scanned the paragraphs.

"This meeting is confidential, right?"

Ethan glanced up at her. "Of course." *Why doesn't she want Libbie to know?*

She squirmed in her chair. "I haven't told my friends what's going on yet."

He set down the agreement and gave her his full attention. "Why not? You know they'll do whatever they can to support you."

"Oh, I know. I don't want to burden them with my issues and I know they'll take this on like it's their own problem to solve."

Ethan shook his head. "Rebecca, your problems aren't a burden to them. What you're going through matters because you matter." He slotted his fingers together and peered at her. "Obviously I won't tell them, but I hope you reconsider. What are friends for if not to offer support in times of crisis?" *Libbie will be so upset to learn she's been shouldering this load by herself.*

"I'll tell them soon, I promise. We have plans to go to Jump!" Instead of meeting them for lunch, Rebecca had suggested they meet at a popular children's activity center to get in touch with their inner child and blow off steam. Within a minute, Kate had responded with YES!, whereas Julie and Libbie had required more convincing.

"Good. Now talk to me about Cloverleaf Critters." Ethan leaned back against his cushioned office chair.

She frowned. "You mean the agreement?"

"No. The shelter itself. I'd like to know more about it. How many dogs come to the shelter each year and how many end up getting adopted? That kind of thing."

Rebecca didn't need to consult any paperwork to answer him. She knew exactly how many dogs had arrived on their doorstep in the past year and how many had been adopted. They weren't simply statistics; each one mattered to her.

"Last year we had 135 dogs placed in homes out of 140. We were also able to find homes for 201 out of 222 cats."

Ethan's eyes widened. "That's wonderful. That's an amazing success rate."

Rebecca squared her shoulders. "Yes, it is. We also help owners recover lost pets. Last year there were fifty-five reported as lost and we helped reunite forty-five of them with their families."

Ethan blew out a breath. "You should be plastering your success all over town. People should know the incredible work you and your staff are doing over there."

Rebecca's eyes turned downcast. "Because I still think about the animals that weren't reunited with their families. I think about the animals still sitting in Cloverleaf Critters, waiting for their forever homes. I've had some animals there for years. There's a wonderful little dog named Odie that's been with us for two years now. He's as sweet as can be, but I've yet to persuade someone to adopt him."

"What do you think the issue is?" he asked.

She plucked the arm of the chair. "I hate to say it, but he's not the most attractive dog in the world. To know him is to love him though. I've considered bringing him home myself, but I'm out of space for another permanent addition."

"That can't be the answer every time you have an animal that doesn't get adopted," he said.

"No, I realize that, which is why I've resigned myself to seeing him at the shelter every day. It still breaks my heart, though. I wish someone would give him a chance." Tears pricked the backs of her eyes and she silently scolded herself for getting emotional. Rebecca had learned it was best to separate her feelings for the animals; otherwise, she risked them getting the better of her.

"Tell me about your budget," Ethan said. "What kind of numbers are we talking about?"

"We're not on the verge of financial collapse, but we're not sitting on a mountain of cash either. The money always goes back into the shelter to serve the animals. We're down 150,000 this year compared with the year before."

"Why is that?"

"The usual," Rebecca said. "People tightening their purse strings. I already let go of one full-time staff member to bridge the gap. I rely on volunteers. Our only source of funding is donations and adoption fees. Right now we're housing more than the average number of animals because of layoffs at the plant before Christmas."

Ethan rubbed his forehead with his thumb. "I didn't even think about the impact that would have on pets."

Rebecca shrugged. "Pets are often the first to go when a family hits a financial snag. These families are worried about where their next meal is coming from. They can't afford to worry about pet care as well." She recalled a particularly heartbreaking moment when a family brought in their black cat to surrender. They must've asked their daughter to wait in the car, but the ten-year-old came bursting through the door weeping. That was a hard day. Salem remained at the shelter and Rebecca hoped the family would be able to get back on their feet soon and reclaim him. The look on that little girl's face still haunted Rebecca's dreams.

"How much are the adoption fees?" Ethan asked. "Any chance of raising them?"

"The fees don't even cover the animal's initial medical expenses. The problem is you don't want to make the fees so high that you dissuade people from adopting. You have to charge something though. I feel like we strike the right balance in terms of cost."

"What about these medical expenses?" Ethan asked. "Do you have a vet on staff?"

Rebecca shook her head. "That would be a huge expense for us. We have a contract with Dr. Nate Moretti, one of the local vets. He provides shelter care at a reduced rate. And we're grateful for that. I feel like we would be hard-pressed to find a better location than the one we already have. That building is equipped for all our needs." She fixed him with a pleading expression. "Is there anything we can do to stop the owner from selling?"

"Legally, I don't see a loophole for you. I'm sorry. Short of buying the building out from under him, I'm not sure that you have any options."

Rebecca frowned. "What if that's what I do then?"

Ethan laughed. "I was only joking about buying the building. You just said your budget is lower than in previous years and your only income is from donations and fees."

An idea began to form in her mind. "What about fundraising?"

"Do you think you can raise that much money in less than five weeks? Your lease's end date is one thing, but once he signs an agreement of sale with another buyer, it won't matter how much money you've raised."

Rebecca's resolve hardened. "It might be a long shot, but I have to try."

Excitement sparked in his eyes. "You're absolutely right. What you do benefits all of Lake Cloverleaf whether people realize it or not. We need to get the word out. Even if you don't make enough to buy the building, at least it would be money to aid with the relocation effort."

Rebecca felt a surge of optimism. She was going to do everything in her power to keep these animals where they were. They'd already been displaced at least once in their lives. She refused to be the reason they were displaced again.

"Thanks for this, Ethan. It's been extremely helpful."

He snorted. "Usually when I give bad news to a client, they don't consider it extremely helpful, but I appreciate the sentiment."

She gathered her belongings. "I need to get over to the elementary school now, but we'll talk again soon. I'm going to need all the help I can get with this."

"Your friends are here for you, Rebecca. Whatever it takes, you know that."

Rebecca gave a crisp nod and rose to her feet. "Whatever it takes."

# CHAPTER NINE

Rebecca stopped by the shelter on the way to school to pick up this week's 'Rosie.' With Ida's blessing, Rebecca had started the Reading with Rosie program a couple years ago to encourage reluctant readers at the elementary school level. The original dog was actually named Rosie, but happily the real Rosie was adopted by one of the families at the school. Rebecca now used the program as an opportunity to show off the different dogs available for adoption. It was a win-win. The kids adored having a dog to read with each week at school and Rebecca was able to promote the shelter animals. Not every dog was the right fit for the program, but there were enough that she was able to rotate them. This week's Rosie was a Jack Russell and poodle mix named Hayward. The little dog was terrific with the young volunteers at the shelter, so Rebecca knew he would be a huge hit with the kids at school.

"Who do we have today?" Lottie asked, as they were buzzed into the building.

"Lottie, I'd like you to meet Hayward." Hayward sat dutifully next to her and looked up at the secretary.

Although Rebecca knew he would be perfectly fine to walk through school without a lead, the principal insisted on taking precautions which Rebecca understood. It would be bad publicity for both of them if something ever went awry.

She guided Hayward down the hall to Mrs. Watson's classroom. The children's excitement was palpable as she entered the room. Mrs. Watson immediately hushed them before they could start chattering, although Rebecca was privy to the elation expressed in their private thoughts. It was, without fail, the highlight of her telepathy thus far. Pure unadulterated joy radiated from their little minds. Rebecca could have stood in the doorway all day and listened to their enthusiasm.

A little girl's arm shut up. "I'm first today! Mrs. Watson said so."

"Nora, do you have your book ready?" the teacher asked.

Nora held up a chapter book.

"You take the beanbag chair," Rebecca instructed. "I'll bring Hayward over to sit with you once you're settled."

No further encouragement was required. Nora scrambled across the floor to the blue beanbag chair in the reading nook. Rebecca walked Hayward across the room and enjoyed the attention of the children. All eyes were fixed on the dog, but they knew to keep their hands to themselves. It never ceased to amaze Rebecca how disciplined children could be when the chance to read with the dog was at stake. Delayed gratification at work.

Nora made herself comfortable on the beanbag chair and opened the book on her lap. Rebecca removed the leash from his collar and ushered Hayward over. The dog instinctively climbed next to the little girl and curled up beside her.

Nora's eyes danced with excitement. "Can I pet him now, please?"

"You may," Rebecca said. "And thank you for asking so nicely."

She left the little girl to have her uninterrupted time with the dog and drifted over to chat with Mrs. Watson. The teacher would have already selected the children for this week's slots. There were too many children for each one to have a turn, so each teacher was responsible for choosing six students per visit. If Rebecca had more staff, she would love to beef up the program. Even if no dogs were adopted as a result, she still felt like it was a worthwhile endeavor for all parties involved. The dogs loved the attention and the children loved giving it to them. Rebecca found that even the staff looked forward to her Reading with Rosie visits.

"How's everything going?" Mrs. Watson asked. She was a veteran teacher and Rebecca never would have guessed she was on the verge of retirement if she hadn't accidentally overheard the woman's thoughts.

"A few bumps in the road at the moment, but I hope to smooth them over," Rebecca said vaguely. She wasn't ready to make an announcement, not until she had more of a plan regarding fundraisers.

"Nora's father left recently, so I know this will cheer her up immensely," Mrs. Watson whispered.

Rebecca's gaze returned to the little girl idly stroking Hayward's head as she read. Teachers were not only instructors, but therapists and sometimes even guardian angels. Nora's happy thoughts made her spirits soar. She couldn't fix the little girl's life, but she could make her feel better for a brief, shining moment.

Rebecca continued to marvel at the children's thoughts. She didn't intend to listen; she just didn't know how to filter out the thoughts yet. What struck her the most was the absence of negativity. No one was worried about chubby thighs or chicken pox scars. Caitlin was concerned about the stuck zipper on her friend's backpack. Billy was happy about baseball season starting. Kayden was awaiting a visit from his grandparents. All of their thoughts seemed so kind and uplifting. When did that change for people? At what age did the swirl of positive thinking morph into a dark cloud? On the one hand, part of the joy of being a child was the lack of responsibility and blissful ignorance. Maybe if adults got back in touch with their inner child, the world would be a happier place. Observing the children now, Rebecca was more convinced than ever that getting in touch with her inner child was the way to inner peace.

"Whose idea was this again?" Rebecca asked as she jumped up and down at the indoor trampoline park. "Oh, that's right. It was mine."

"I'm glad I wore a bra," Julie said. "My boobs would have blinded me by now from smacking me in the eye one too many times."

Kate laughed as she performed a flip and landed gracefully on her feet. "I think this is fun. I used to come here with the kids when they were younger. It never occurred to me to jump with them."

"Probably for the best," Libbie said. "You would've ended up competing with them for best backward flip anyway."

Kate jumped into a spread-eagle position and landed on her butt, immediately bouncing back onto her feet like a pro. "This is amazing core work."

"I miss the treadmill," Rebecca said. "I can still breathe on there."

Kate gave her a pointed look. "Then you're not doing it right."

"Look at me upside down," Julie called. "I've had a free

facelift." With her head tipped back, Julie hung over the edge of the raised trampoline.

"Coming here now was genius," Kate said. "The only people here are moms with toddlers."

Rebecca glanced over at the neighboring section where a trio of mothers sat observing their bouncing offspring. The moment she focused on them, one of their thoughts penetrated her mind.

*They're bouncing too close together. One of them is going to hurt themselves. With my luck, it'll be Annie. She'll bang her head against one of the others and get a concussion and then I'll have to take her to the emergency room, which means a twenty-dollar playdate ends up costing five-hundred dollars.*

Rebecca sympathized. It couldn't be easy letting your children learn to walk through the world independently. It was as much of a rite of passage for the parent as the child. Her own parents hadn't been overly involved in her childhood, so she doubted they'd experienced too many fears and concerns when it came to Rebecca. They lived separate lives from early on. Rebecca's activities were solely for her. They dropped her off and picked her up from soccer and softball games, but they didn't hang around to cheer like some of the other parents. She hadn't given it much thought at the time. It was just the way things were.

"I'm surprised you'd want to go to any public places until you get used to your gift," Kate said. "How are you not in constant agony?"

Rebecca had shared the news of her telepathy with Kate and Julie on the way to Jump! and her friends had barraged her with questions.

"I think the second recipe in the book is there to help me retain my sanity," Rebecca said. "It isn't complete chaos in my head." She paused. "Well, that's not strictly true. There are other things making me crazy."

"Other things like what?" Kate asked.

"I have a pretty big problem," Rebecca announced, slightly out of breath from jumping. She slowed to a slow bounce before she hurt herself. She couldn't afford to be out of commission now.

Julie bolted back to an upright position. "What's wrong?"

Rebecca felt a pang of guilt for kicking off the conversation this way. Julie's mind probably went straight to cancer because of her experience with Greg.

"I'm not sick or anything," Rebecca said quickly. She told them about the sale of the building. "So I need ideas for fundraisers so the shelter can buy the building."

"What's the name of the owner?" Kate asked. "Maybe he's someone Lucas deals with."

"Brian Shea, and I can promise you that a word from God wouldn't matter to this man. He is all about the Benjamins."

"Have you looked at other options?" Julie asked. "Maybe there's a building you can lease that would actually work better for you."

"I've been working with MaryAnn, actually," Rebecca said. "She's doing her best, but I'm not hopeful the ideal building exists. Our needs are so specific and it would be much less hassle to stay put."

Rebecca stepped off the trampoline to take a break from bouncing.

"Cramp!" Libbie proclaimed. She whimpered as she vacated the trampoline and squeezed her shoulder.

"Here. Let me massage it for you," Rebecca said. "It's the least I can do since I dragged you here."

"That's the spot right there," Libbie said.

Rebecca could feel the hard knot that had formed just above the shoulder blade. She dug her knuckles in, prompting a moan of relief from Libbie.

"I'd be happy to cater something for you," Libbie said. "You could host a luncheon with a raffle."

"A raffle isn't going to be enough to buy a building downtown," Rebecca said, "not that I don't appreciate the offer."

"Then we should host a grander affair," Kate said.

Leave it to Kate to come up with a fancy alternative. "What do you propose, madam? A masquerade ball?" Rebecca joked.

"And hide this face? Never," Kate said. "We could have a Memorial Day barbecue with a silent auction component." Inspiration flickered in her blue eyes. "We'll make it the event of the season. Libbie will have an upmarket menu like Kobe beef burgers with bleu cheese and we'll only allow a certain number of attendees to make it feel exclusive. The harder something is to get tickets for, the more people want them. It's human nature."

Julie looked at her. "I'd be happy to host at my house. It would be a great way to introduce the B&B to the community. And if it's exclusive then I know I'll have enough space. We could hold the silent auction inside and the barbecue outside."

Rebecca warmed to the idea. Julie's house had the best view of the lake in town. People would love to spend Memorial Day basking lakeside in the sun with flutes of prosecco and fancy burgers.

"I love this," Rebecca enthused. "You have no idea how much it means to have your support."

Kate bounced her way off the trampoline and nailed the landing. "We'll need donations for the silent auction. Why don't you leave that part to me? Lucas has some high-end clients with great connections. Concert tickets. Sporting events. You name it and we can come up with something bidders will pay top-dollar for."

Libbie pointed to a sign by the office door. "They hold

fundraisers here too." She squinted to read the smaller print. "Looks like your organization would get a percentage of every entry fee for the event."

Julie brightened. "You could have two fundraisers here. One for kids to jump and a second one that's adults only."

"Do you have a GoFundMe page set up?" Kate asked. "If not, I highly recommend it. I can post the link on all my social media platforms for you."

"You're the best friends a woman could ask for," Rebecca said. She felt so much better now; she wished she'd told them sooner instead of keeping it to herself and creating more stress.

"And you're the best friend those animals could ask for," Kate said. "Too bad you can't hear their thoughts to know how much they appreciate you."

"Seriously though, what is the point of telepathy?" Rebecca lamented. "The only purpose it serves is to torture me."

"That's not true. I heard you tell that woman in the lobby that she didn't look fat in her yoga pants," Libbie said. "That's basically a public service."

"She'll remember it for two seconds and then go back to criticizing herself," Rebecca argued. "It's a worthless gift."

Julie bounced on her toes. "I thought my gift was awful at first, remember? But I've learned something from every ghost I've met."

Kate arched an eyebrow. "Make sure you're wearing a flattering outfit when you die?"

"Well, that," Julie admitted, "but each one also had an attitude adjustment after they died. An aha! moment."

"Each mind shift is an opportunity to learn and grow," Libbie said. "To heal."

"Hard to heal when you're already dead," Kate said.

"How can eavesdropping on people's private thoughts

result in an attitude adjustment?" Rebecca asked. "If they're already thinking it, then they're already aware of it."

Julie barked a short laugh. "Are you aware every time you call yourself stupid or incompetent in your head?"

"Or fat," Libbie added.

Rebecca realized they were right. She'd been astounded when she'd heard her thoughts repeated back to her by Iago. It would likely be the same with other people whose thoughts she overheard. Negative self-talk seemed to be on autopilot. They'd probably been making the same negative remarks to themselves for most of their lives without being fully conscious of it.

"Speaking of fat, I think I've lost five pounds since we've been here," Libbie said. "We should make this a regular outing."

"If we're all so thrilled by this outing, then why am I the only one left jumping?" Julie asked, continuing to bounce.

Rebecca rejoined her friend on the trampoline. "You're not alone anymore, but you'll probably wish you were when I smack into you."

The thoughts of the neighboring mothers pushed through the sound of her laughter.

*What a spectacle*, one of the women thought. *They're too old to be behaving like children.*

*They should be embarrassed. They look ridiculous.*

*I hope I don't act like that when I'm their age.* She paused. *Although I wouldn't mind looking as good as the blonde. I'd never worry about Brandon leaving me if I looked like that. She must've had a mommy makeover. I hear they're all the rage for older women.*

*I don't think that one is wearing a bra. Her boobs are swinging like melons in the wind.*

"More like lemons," Rebecca muttered.

The more comments Rebecca overheard, the more her

good mood began to deflate. Her positive outlook for the shelter was now usurped by the negative remarks. Wordlessly, she stepped off the trampoline.

"Hey," Julie called. "Where're you going?"

"I feel a twinge in my back. I think I should stop now." Rebecca hated to lie, but she didn't want to share the misery. Let her friends remain blissfully ignorant like the children in Mrs. Watson's classroom. It was better that way.

# CHAPTER TEN

Rebecca stood in the backyard of Danielle Putnam's house, holding a red rubber ball. Max, the energetic Siberian husky, watched her carefully with his ice blue eyes. Rebecca adored huskies, but she could understand why Danielle was feeling overwhelmed. The woman's previous dog had been a West Highland terrier whose favorite activity was snuggling on the sofa. Huskies were originally bred to be sled dogs, which meant long-distance running and endurance. Max's active personality must've come as a shock to her.

Rebecca tossed the ball as far as she could and prayed she didn't pull a muscle. It had happened two years ago at a Labor Day picnic when she'd agreed to join an impromptu softball game. Rebecca had been athletic in her younger years and was surprised to find she couldn't throw a ball as easily as she once had. In fact, middle age had taken her by surprise in general. She'd heard the warnings, of course, but she'd disregarded them. They were for 'old people' or 'people who didn't take care of themselves.' She regretted that attitude now. She knew firsthand that some aspects of middle age happened whether you took care of yourself or not.

"He's so fast," Danielle said. "If he ever decides to jump the fence and make a run for it, there's no way I'll catch him."

"That's one reason training is so important. You put yourself at the top of the hierarchy and he'll come when you call."

Danielle folded her arms. "I don't even put myself at the top of the hierarchy for me. I'm not sure I can do it for a dog."

Rebecca understood the sentiment. "Spoken like a true woman."

"He's so sweet and affectionate." She laughed. "I wish I could meet a man with half his positive traits."

Rebecca smiled. "Amen, sister."

Danielle lit up. "Oh, you're single too?"

Rebecca held up her left hand. "Never even had a ring. How about you?"

"Recently divorced," Danielle said. "Our son Trevor is in college now."

"I'm sorry to hear that. Not about college, of course. That's great."

She wore a sad smile. "Empty nest syndrome. It's like erecting a spotlight where your kid used to be. Shines a bright light on all the cracks in the relationship."

Rebecca didn't know what to say. She'd heard that divorce was common once kids grew up and left the nest, but she had no personal experience with it. Her parents had maintained a strong bond throughout her childhood. It only stood to reason that their relationship would withstand an empty nest. In fact, Rebecca was fairly certain they'd looked forward to her departure the same way a high school student ticks down the days to graduation.

*Boundaries, Danielle. You just met her. She doesn't need to hear all the details of your life.*

"I'm sorry it didn't work out," Rebecca said, "but you made a good choice with Max. He seems like a great dog."

Danielle glanced with affection at the husky, who was now running back and forth across the yard at top speed. "Looks like he's got a case of the zoomies."

"That usually happens indoors at my house. Outside would be better." Sugar had gotten herself so worked up one time that she'd crashed into the wall. She was sweet but not always smart. "Huskies are pack dogs, which means Max will try to challenge your leadership and test your boundaries."

"Oh, so he's like Trevor's early teen years." Danielle rolled her eyes. "Man, I don't miss those days."

"He needs a lot of exercise," Rebecca continued. "Definitely more than your previous dog used to get."

"How do I know what he considers enough?"

Rebecca gave her a pointed look. "Max will let you know. He'll be destructive and generally unhappy. My advice is to have him outside as much as you can manage." She hesitated. "I don't mean leave him outside all day unattended."

Danielle pulled a face. "No, I would never. I figure it'll be good for me to be out here with him. Keep me from moping in the house."

"Good plan," Rebecca said. "It's nice to see that happy face when you come home too." She turned to smile at Max, who now had the ball clenched in his jaws and was shaking his head with abandon. He really was a gorgeous dog. Once he calmed down, Danielle was going to be so grateful for his company.

"I really appreciate you doing this," Danielle said. "I was searching online to hire someone, but then Peter mentioned hearing you talk at the library and you were so knowledgeable."

Rebecca waved her off. "Don't mention it. Huskies are notoriously difficult to train, not because they're bad, of course." She crouched down to give the dog a vigorous pat on the back as he raced over to them for attention. "Who's a good boy? That's right. You are."

"For a second, I thought you were talking to me."

Rebecca's head swiveled to see Peter opening the gate to the backyard and her stomach executed a somersault. In a snug T-shirt, jeans, and flip-flops, he looked even better than at the library.

"Hey, I didn't expect to see you today." Danielle crossed the lawn to give her brother a hug, but Max decided to cut in line. The dog jumped up and landed his dirty paws on Peter's thighs.

"Down, boy," Peter said firmly.

Max dropped his paws and Peter dusted off his jeans.

"Why does he listen to you so easily?" Danielle complained.

He held out his arms. "Because testosterone courses through these veins."

He wasn't wrong. "Like I said, huskies respond to a hierarchy," Rebecca said. "That's why I was telling you earlier to make clear who's in charge."

Peter bent over to stroke the dog's head. "Sounds like you're learning a thing or two."

*I hope so. There's no way I'd want to give back a dog after adopting him.*

Despite Danielle's concerns, Rebecca wasn't worried about her. She could tell the woman was committed to training Max and the dog wasn't really challenging. It was more about an attitude adjustment—for both of them. Rebecca smiled to herself, remembering the conversation at Jump! with her friends. A simple attitude adjustment really could make all the difference.

"She's going to be great," Rebecca said, hoping to reassure Danielle without letting her know she could read her thoughts.

"Well, she's a great mom to Trevor, so I can't claim to be surprised," Peter said.

"Trevor might offer an alternative opinion," Danielle said.

"I'll be sure to ask him the next time he comes home to ask you to do his laundry," Peter teased.

Rebecca laughed. "Not such an empty nest after all, is it?"

"He'll be home for Memorial Day weekend," Danielle said. "That's one of the reasons I was hoping to get help with Max. I don't want Trevor to think I can't handle it. I don't need a lecture from my own son."

Peter's thoughts cut straight through the conversation. *How can I do this so that I don't make a complete ass out of myself? Danielle will never let me hear the end of it.*

Rebecca was careful not to look at him. What was it that he wanted to do? Something with Max, like a trick? Or something to do with Trevor's visit?

"I should probably head out," Rebecca said. If he wanted to play with the dog without fear of criticism by the 'expert,' then Rebecca would get out of his way.

His face registered surprise. "Oh, so soon? I didn't mean to break up the party."

"Rebecca has been more than gracious with her time," Danielle said. "Max and I appreciate it."

Peter raked a hand through his long hair. "Let me walk you to your car."

Rebecca laughed. "It's only right there in the driveway." She gestured toward the gate.

"Then it won't be a big deal for me to walk you there," he said.

*Pick up on the social cues, single lady*, Danielle thought.

Oh, wow. Peter was trying to get her alone? Rebecca was both thrilled and terrified. Was he genuinely interested in her? She didn't seem like his type, not that she had any idea what his type was. Just because she had a thing for long-haired sensitive souls didn't mean the reverse was true.

They walked in companionable silence until they reached her car.

"Would you be interested in going out with me next weekend?" he blurted. *Cool, Peter. Way to sound like you've never been on a date before.*

A cocoon burst in Rebecca's stomach, releasing butterflies everywhere. "I would love to, but I've got a big fundraiser to plan for Memorial Day and I think it's going to consume all my time."

"Ah, the old fundraiser excuse," he said, his head bobbing. "I completely understand." *Okay, she's not interested.*

Rebecca's heart skipped a beat. She didn't want him to think that. "I'm sure I can steal an hour or so for myself though," she said.

He beamed. "Terrific. How about dinner Saturday night then? You have to eat, right?"

Rebecca debated whether to counter with a lunch date like she normally would, but Peter seemed different. For starters, she wasn't meeting him online. She felt confident she'd make it through dinner with him relatively unscathed.

"Saturday night sounds great."

*Thank God*, he thought. *For a second there, I thought she was going to turn me down.*

"I'll call you with the details." He paused. "Or text you, if you prefer. I know not everyone likes to talk on the phone. I'm fine with either."

Rebecca smiled. "So am I." She opened the door and slid behind the wheel, her excitement rising. She had a date with a handsome adult male who lived with two cats and arranged dog training for his sister. Peter Putnam seemed like a real catch.

So why did he want to go out with her?

Rebecca tried to shove down the thought, but each time she allowed herself a moment of joyful anticipation, the negativity pushed its way back to the surface. By the time she arrived home, she was in a bad mood and her head was starting to throb. Somewhere between Danielle's house and her own, she managed to convince herself that he had some ulterior motive for asking her out. Never mind that it made no sense. Deep down Rebecca believed she wasn't worthy of his attention and so there had to be another explanation.

She opened the door and was pleased when the animals swarmed to greet her. The cats called loudly for their food, except Angelica who had better manners. She didn't even mind the wet patch on the carpet that was Sugar's way of objecting to her tardiness. The animals loved her unconditionally and would never reject her. Home was safe.

Rebecca nuzzled Sugar's nose and returned to an upright position. "Who wants to go out?"

The dogs barked in unison and followed her to the back door. Her body relaxed as she opened the door and watched them scatter. Their needs were so simple and pure and they were so easy to please.

Leaning her head against the doorjamb, she watched them burn off energy. She'd focus on the animals and what they needed. If nothing else, it was much easier than focusing on herself.

# CHAPTER ELEVEN

"How many tickets have we sold so far?" Libbie asked.

The four friends were gathered in Julie's kitchen for a fundraising meeting. And Peggy, the fourth of Inga's cats, was resting peacefully on the windowsill, occasionally flicking her tail in response to something they said.

"All of them. We're sold out," Kate said.

Julie shook her head as though she'd misheard. "Wait, what? Are you serious?"

"Sold. Out," Kate repeated. "Do I look like an amateur to you? Do you know how many school fundraisers and Girl Scout cookies I have under my belt?"

Rebecca was amazed. Part of her had worried they'd started too close to the event to hit their goal, but Kate had been right about the scarcity tactic. The more coveted something seemed, the more people wanted it.

"Any updates from MaryAnn?" Julie asked.

Rebecca heaved a weary sigh. "Only to say that she's still looking, but there aren't many lease options available right now in general."

"What about a cheaper building to buy?" Libbie asked. "Maybe you could reduce your fundraising goal."

"The cost of renovating a cheaper building…It would just end up costing the same as buying the building we're in," Rebecca explained. "Not to mention the disruption to the animals. I can't put a price tag on that."

"I looked at a few buildings for sale online and the cheaper options were more rural," Kate added. "You don't want to be isolated, especially in the winter."

"Now I'm picturing The Shining," Julie said, shuddering. "Thanks for that."

Kate placed her hands on the counter. "Let's fine-tune the details for Monday. We can offer our suggestions through the lost art of miming and the others have to guess."

"Miming is a lost art for a reason," Libbie said. "Mimes are creepy."

"Are we seriously going to play Charades?" Julie asked, her gaze flitting from one friend to the next.

"You only want to make it a competition," Rebecca accused.

Kate offered a weak smile. "It'll be more fun that way."

"For you, maybe," Julie shot back. "The rest of us mere mortals would prefer cocktails and conversation minus the competition."

"I hate to break it to you, but I can read your minds," Rebecca said, "which means I'd win without breaking a sweat."

Kate frowned. "A point I failed to consider."

"We don't have time for games anyway," Rebecca said. "We have too much to do for Monday."

Kate made a calming gesture with her hands. "It's under control."

Rebecca flicked a hand in the direction of the living room. "Does that look like it's under control to you?"

The folding table they'd set up in Julie's living room was covered in an assortment of objects and sheets of paper. Nothing was organized.

"It'll be fine," Libbie reassured her. "Everything will be set up well in advance of the event."

"I'm the one who has to stare at the mess," Julie said. "Not that I'm complaining. All for a good cause." She forced a cheerful smile.

"I'd like to hear more about this Peter Putnam," Libbie said, eyeing Rebecca curiously.

"We're here to talk about the fundraiser," Rebecca reminded them, her cheeks starting to burn.

"Can't we do both?" Libbie asked.

"He has a website," Kate practically shrieked.

Suddenly Rebecca was sixteen again and her friends had discovered an old yearbook with a crush's photo.

Kate turned the laptop so they could all see the screen.

Julie whistled. "Holy smokin'. You left out how extremely hot he is."

"He makes furniture?" Libbie asked. "How cool."

Rebecca thought so too. She'd already seen the website when she'd Googled him in the privacy of her own home.

"He makes it by hand." Kate fanned herself. "Imagine what he can do with his hands when he's not polishing knobs."

Rebecca groaned. "I knew I should've kept this to myself. We haven't even been on a date yet."

"And you met him in person and not online?" Julie asked, her gaze pinned to the image on the screen.

"He dropped in during my library talk," Rebecca said. "Asked me to help with his sister's dog."

Kate rolled her eyes. "Oh, the help-my-sister's-dog excuse. One of the oldest tricks in the book."

"Danielle's really nice and the dog is terrific."

"It's good to get along with your sister-in-law," Libbie teased.

Rebecca pressed her lips together. She could tell they were having too much fun to stop anytime soon. If you can't beat 'em, join 'em.

She leaned forward to study the screen. "His work is incredible."

"What kind of furniture does he make?" Julie asked.

"Tables, chairs, hope chests, decorative crates." Kate clicked through the website.

"I'd love a hope chest to store my mother's things," Julie said.

Kate's eyes sparkled. "We should ask him to donate something to the silent auction."

"It's on Monday," Rebecca objected. "We can't ask on such short notice."

"Maybe he has a commissioned piece sitting there that a client backed out on," Kate said, sounding quite reasonable. "You never know."

Rebecca admired his handsome face on the screen. "I don't want to ask him for a favor before we've even been on a date. It's tacky."

"I agree with Rebecca," Libbie said. "If they were already dating it would be one thing, but they barely know each other."

Kate clicked on the link for 'About Me.' "Says here he's been woodworking since he was thirteen. He likes long hikes in the woods and his favorite ice cream is pistachio. There. Now you know him."

Rebecca grabbed the screen and turned it toward her. "It does not!"

"Okay, maybe not the rest, but the first sentence is true," Kate admitted.

"He found the thing he loves to do and made it his career," Libbie said. "So we know he's in touch with himself."

"And now he can spend the rest of his life touching you," Kate said, nudging her.

Rebecca covered her ears. "Can we get back to the fundraiser? I feel like Peter is an extra layer of stress I don't need right now."

Julie squeezed her shoulder. "Try to see him as a welcome opportunity."

Rebecca cocked a skeptical eyebrow. "Because that's how you saw David when you first met him?" Julie had been vehemently opposed to dating when she met David, a middle-aged doctor, at his father's apartment. Rebecca had accompanied her there at the request of a ghost with unfinished business. David had clearly expressed an interest in Julie, but she was too stuck in grief over her husband's death to consider dating another man. Communicating with Greg's ghost had given Julie the strength she needed to move on.

"It's not the same situation and you know it," Julie said. "But I can understand wanting to stay focused on the shelter issue. The stakes are pretty high."

"No kidding." Rebecca glanced at the table for the silent auction. "Why don't we start organizing the items and choosing starting bids?"

"Can we go over the menu first?" Libbie asked. "I want to confirm a few small changes. I couldn't get the amount of shrimp I needed so I've swapped one of the appetizers."

"Whatever you decide is fine with me," Rebecca said. "You're the chef."

Libbie beamed. "I am, aren't I?" She clapped her hands. "Have I mentioned lately how much I love my job?"

"Only a million times in the past year," Kate said. She sauntered over to the table and inspected the items at the end. "Nick donated an ice cream party, Libbie? That's such a great idea."

Libbie's ex-husband owned a local ice cream parlor that was one of the most popular places in town once the heat rolled in.

"He was happy to pitch in," Libbie said. "You know he loves animals." She and Nick shared custody of their kids as well as their dog.

Rebecca peered over Kate's shoulder at the list now in her hand. "I didn't even notice those Eagles tickets. Who donated those?"

"A friend of Lucas," Kate said. "He has season tickets."

Rebecca was floored by the generosity of the donations. Flyers tickets. 76'ers. Phillies. All the major sports were represented. There were museum memberships, a shopping spree at the local bookstore, a salon makeover, a catered dinner party from Libbie, and a stay at the B&B from Julie.

"Do you really think this is going to work?" Rebecca asked.

Kate set the list back on the table. "I think you're off to a roaring start."

"I wish I had more time," Rebecca said. "I feel like he deliberately waited until the very end of the notice period to spring this on me."

Libbie nodded. "Ethan said the same thing. Brian Shea doesn't have a great reputation in the business community."

"No surprise there," Rebecca grumbled.

"The weekend weather forecast looks perfect," Kate said. "This is going to get us partway to your goal, Rebecca. We just need to come up with a few more gems like this and we're golden."

Rebecca snorted. "You had to sneak that in didn't you, Mrs. Golden?"

Kate shrugged. "It fit the occasion."

Dread coiled in Rebecca's stomach as she gazed at the table. If she failed to pull this off, she doubted there'd be enough time to plan another huge event. She needed this fundraiser to do the bulk of the heavy lifting or she might as well start finding alternate shelters for the animals.

Memorial Day couldn't come soon enough.

Rebecca left the fundraising meeting and drove straight to her next appointment. She parked in the driveway of a modest split-level home in one of the neighborhoods on the eastern edge of town. The Morris family had completed the paperwork to adopt Magnus, one of the shelter's more active dogs. The Labrador mix was going to require a lot of playtime, but Rebecca felt confident that Harry and Alyssa Morris and their two kids were up to the challenge.

One of the tasks on Rebecca's checklist involved a pre-adoption home visit. Although she didn't anticipate any issues with the Morris family, the home visit was a requirement before they'd be able to keep Magnus permanently.

The front door opened before she made it to the front step and the Morris's thirteen-year-old twins bounced on the balls of their feet, excited for her arrival. Their thoughts were a jumble of words that included *happy* and *excited*. Rebecca couldn't decide which one was more thrilled to be adopting Magnus.

The dog came barreling toward her, his tongue hanging out of the side of his mouth. He was one of those good-natured dogs that always looked like he was smiling.

"Hey, Magnus." Rebecca grabbed his snout and nuzzled it. The dog licked her face in return.

Justin turned and called for his parents. Rebecca never tired of this part of the job. She loved the feeling of acceptance that came with an animal's new home. The Morris family had welcomed Magnus with open arms, she knew that much.

Mrs. Morris appeared in the foyer with her husband. "Welcome, Rebecca. Come on in."

Rebecca observed the family's interactions with the dog. Nobody was too rough or too stern. They were a natural fit and all their thoughts seemed to express the hope that Magnus could stay.

"As you can see, we're all very glad you're here to make it official," Mrs. Morris said. "Can I get you anything to eat or drink?"

"No, thank you. If you wouldn't mind giving me a little tour, I'd love to see a-day-in-the-life-of Magnus."

Alyssa Morris guided her to the upstairs level and inclined her head toward the first bedroom. "I think Magnus is going to have his pick of beds. The kids have already been creating their own sleepover schedule. They promised to take turns and not fight." She rolled her eyes. "We'll see how long that lasts."

"Magnus isn't exactly a small dog," Rebecca said. "They might regret that decision."

"We all have queen-sized beds," she said. "The only bed I prefer he stay off of is mine, but Murphy's Law says it will be his favorite place to sleep."

She didn't seem genuinely bothered by that prospect. She took Rebecca through the rest of the house and showed her where the dog would stay when no one was home, which was rare because Mrs. Morris worked from home.

Next they went to the backyard where Rebecca checked for secure fencing and looked for any signs of a previously chained dog like a stake in the ground. She knew she wouldn't find one, but it was her duty to check. She would only leave the dog permanently with new companions when she was satisfied they'd take good care of him. She had no qualms about the Morris family.

As they returned to the house, she felt Mrs. Morris's eyes on her. "You assessed my house the way I used to assess strange places before I'd leave my kids there," she said. "You must be a mother."

"Only to the animals," Rebecca replied.

"Well, take it from this mama bear, you'd make one hell of a mother." Mrs. Morris glanced in the direction of the dog, now running around the backyard with the kids. "You've done a great job taking care of him. We'd be happy to take it from here. Free up space for another deserving dog with boundless energy."

"Well, he's all yours," Rebecca said. "I'll sign off on the paperwork and email you a copy."

"That's great news," Mrs. Morris said, visibly relieved. "I have a feeling we might be back to take another one off your hands once this one has settled in. Give Magnus a playmate when we're all too worn out for him." She laughed.

"If you decide to adopt again, I think I have the perfect dog."

Mrs. Morris looked at her sideways. "I'm listening."

"He's a Doberman named Paul Rudd. I actually think a dog like Magnus might be a good playmate for him." Rebecca frowned. "That's assuming we haven't had to ship him off to another shelter by then."

Mrs. Morris raised her eyebrows. "Why would you need to do that?" *Does he not get along with the other animals at the shelter?*

"Because the owner of the building has exercised his right to sell and I haven't been able to find a suitable location for us. Unfortunately the clock is ticking and I doubt the right space is going to magically appear in time."

Mrs. Morris pursed her lips in consternation. "That's awful. Is there anything we can do?"

Rebecca didn't know what to say. She knew the Morris family wasn't flush with cash and she wanted them to save their extra money for Magnus and, hopefully, Paul Rudd.

"We're going to be hosting fundraisers over the next few weeks. If you could help spread the word, that would be great."

"If you need help with flyers or anything at all, please let me know. Our whole family would love to help."

"Thank you. I will." Again, Rebecca felt better once she'd unburdened herself. People didn't seem to blame her for the shelter's predicament and were eager to help. She had to keep reminding herself of that.

As she ducked back into her car, she heard Mrs. Morris echo Libbie's words from the night of cocktail club—

*It takes a village.*

# CHAPTER TWELVE

By the time Saturday night rolled around, Rebecca felt surprisingly nervous about her date with Peter. She wasn't sure whether it was because she hadn't chatted online with him for weeks in advance like she typically did with a date or because she found him so attractive. There was, of course, the nagging voice in the back of her mind that said this was too good to be true. She did her best to silence that voice, but it wasn't easy.

He'd offered to pick her up at her house, which Rebecca usually didn't allow. As a single woman who lived alone, she'd made a rule about letting strange men know where she lived. For some reason, she'd accepted Peter's offer without a second thought.

She was adjusting a wayward curl when she heard a knock on the door. Naturally the dogs went wild. The man with two cats obviously didn't realize the effect his knock would have on her brood. She hurried to the door with a parade of animals behind her.

She cracked open the door. "Hi. I'm about ready. Do you

want to come in for a second or would you rather avoid the attack of the tongues?"

His brow lifted. "I feel like tongue attacks should come at the end of a date."

She laughed as he wedged his way through the crack to join her in the kitchen. She knew she could sweep the animals out of sight to make him more comfortable, but she was curious to see how he interacted with them.

"I think they smell AC and DC," Peter said, crouching to their level and rubbing every head placed within reach.

Rebecca was pleased the animals seemed to approve. Looking at him now, she did as well. He wore a white button-down collared shirt unbuttoned at the top and bottom with the sleeves rolled up just enough to offer a glimpse of powerful forearms, paired with dark blue jeans. His hair appeared slightly damp from the shower and he smelled like fresh soap. With the way he looked and smelled, it was hard not to picture him in the shower.

"Rebecca," he said, looking at her closely.

She snapped back to reality. "Yes? What?"

"I asked if you were ready," he said, smiling. "It's the holiday weekend so I have no doubt they'll give our table away if we're not there close enough to our reservation time."

She grabbed her purse from the kitchen counter. "All set."

*She looks amazing.* "You look amazing," he said.

"Thank you." She'd chosen a black cotton dress that hugged her curves but didn't seem too fancy for the occasion.

She stepped outside and spotted his pickup truck parked behind her car.

"Hope you don't mind the truck," he said, as though reading her mind for a change. "It's a little higher off the ground, but I can give you a boost if you need it."

He walked her to the passenger-side door and opened it for her.

"I'll manage." She pulled herself up and into the seat without incident.

A moment later, he slid into the driver's seat beside her. "I use this to haul pieces of furniture. Couldn't run my business without it."

"Oh?" She feigned ignorance, not wanting to seem like a creeper. "What kind of business?"

"Woodworking. I make furniture," he said, backing out of the driveway and turning onto the road.

"That's pretty impressive."

"Love it. Can't imagine doing anything else," he said.

"Me neither," Rebecca said.

He glanced at her and smiled. "Sounds like we're both content with our livelihoods. Time to make room for a relationship, right?" *Too soon, Peter. You don't throw around the 'r' word like a Frisbee.*

Rebecca's stomach tightened as her butterflies clustered together. There was something decidedly intimate about riding in the truck with him and she felt both exhilarated and terrified.

"I'm sure you've been to The Cove," he said, as they arrived at the northern side of the lake. This area of Lake Cloverleaf was more secluded, which was why The Cove was known for its romantic setting.

"I've been once or twice," she said. Once for an engagement party and once for Kate's birthday dinner. "It's a great choice. I can't believe you got reservations on a holiday weekend."

"I made a few pieces for the owner," he said. "I may have pulled a string or two."

He parked the truck and was quick to arrive at her door to help her to the ground. Rebecca's short stature generally wasn't an issue except when it came to high shelves or gracefully exiting a monster truck.

"Thanks," she said, relieved when both feet landed squarely on the concrete parking lot.

"It's a beautiful night," he said. "Any objection to a table outside?"

Rebecca brightened. "Not at all. I love dining under the stars."

"Glad to hear it. So do I." He approached the hostess stand and Rebecca noticed a slight swagger to his walk. "Hi there. We have a reservation for two under Putnam."

The hostess smiled. "Welcome to The Cove. Your table is ready, Mr. Putnam. Tanya will take you there."

Rebecca thought the restaurant looked particularly festive this evening with strings of delicate fairy lights and live music playing in the background. It was just the right volume —loud enough to hear, but not so loud they wouldn't be able to enjoy their conversation.

Tanya arrived at a table closest to the pier and waited until they were seated to hand them each a menu.

"Thank you, Tanya," he said.

The young woman blushed. "You probably don't remember me. You made my little brother's baseball bat. His name's Timmy."

Peter's face lit up in recognition. "Yes, of course. His tenth birthday, right?"

"That's right." She seemed shocked that he remembered.

"Tell him hey for me, will you?"

She tugged on a strand of hair. "Definitely." She seemed to remember her role tonight. "The specials are on the insert. Anything to drink while you look over the menu?"

Peter glanced at her. "Bottle of wine? Beer? Iced tea?"

"What will you have?"

"I'm the chauffeur so I'll stick to one beer tonight." He turned to Tanya. "Whatever's on tap."

Rebecca ordered a prosecco. It was light enough that she'd have plenty of room for food and not enough alcohol to get her drunk.

"I'll be back with those in a minute," Tanya said.

"That's so cute that you remember her brother's baseball bat," Rebecca said, once Tanya was out of earshot.

"Hard to forget that bat," he said. "I worked on it nonstop until it was finished. The parents left his present a little late and paid extra to have it done in time for his party."

Rebecca didn't need to study the menu to know what she wanted. One of the perks of having a friend for a chef was learning the best dishes to order. Over the course of the past year, Libbie had given them a primer on every restaurant in town including The Cove.

"What are your thoughts on appetizers?" he asked, peering at her over the top of his menu.

Rebecca was startled by the isolated view of his eyes. With thick lashes and flecks of gold in the green irises, she'd failed to notice how striking his eyes were until now. She was so distracted that she completely forgot to answer his question.

"Rebecca?"

She straightened in her seat. "Huh?"

He turned the menu toward her. "Any appetizers jumping out at you?"

"Oh. Right." She closed her menu. "My friend Libbie is a top-notch chef and she says to skip the apps here and go for a main and a dessert."

Peter didn't object. Copying her movements, he closed his menu. "Did she have an opinion on the fish tacos here?"

Rebecca's mouth curved into a gentle smile. "That's what I'm having."

"Extra guac for me," he said.

Tanya returned to the table with their drinks and took their order for two fish tacos for the main course.

"What's this big event on Memorial Day?" he asked.

She told him about the fundraiser and the reason it was needed.

He whistled. "That blows. I'm sorry. I assume you spoke to a lawyer to see if there was anything you could do."

She nodded. "I've been working with a realtor too, but there's nothing yet."

"What happens if you don't raise enough money and you can't find an alternate lease?"

She lowered her gaze. "Then we have to hurry up and find homes for all the animals."

"But if you haven't found them homes already, you're not going to suddenly have people lining up to take them, are you?"

A lump formed in her throat. No. No, she would not. "I could divide them up and farm them out to different no-kill shelters. It's not ideal."

He swigged his beer. "Also sounds like a lot of grunt work."

"I don't mind grunt work," she said. "I mind uprooting them."

"Why don't more people foster?"

She turned her gaze to the moonlight that now rippled across the water. It really was a beautiful evening. "It's a lot of work. I also think they're afraid to get too attached and then have to face giving up the animal."

He pondered her response. "I guess I can understand their fear. It's like embarking on a new relationship. You don't know how things will pan out, so it makes you too nervous to even put yourself out there in the first place."

Rebecca turned back to him and smiled. "You sound like Julie."

"Friend of yours?"

Rebecca nodded. "She refused to join any dating sites or wade into the dating pool in any way after her husband died."

"Can't say I blame her about the sites. I don't use them either."

"How do you meet anyone?"

His mouth quirked. "Where else? The library."

She laughed. "So I'm not the first woman you checked out at the library."

He wagged a finger at her. "I see what you did there." His smile faded. "I guess I'm like your friend. Not much of a dater." *Danielle said I'm not supposed to admit that. Makes me sound like a recluse.*

"Ever been married?" she asked.

"Once."

"How long?"

"Four years, although we'd been together for a long time before we actually tied the knot." *Because I knew we weren't right for each other, but I was too afraid to admit it.*

"Do you think that's why it took so long to commit? Because part of you sensed it wasn't right?"

He shot her a quizzical look. "Yeah, I'd say that about sums it up." He took another swig of beer. "How about you? Is there an ex-husband you'd like to have in voodoo doll form, so you know where to stick your pins?"

She laughed again. "No, I've managed to get to my forties without a wedding ceremony, although I was briefly engaged once."

His eyebrow shot up. "Is that so? What happened?"

"We were seven. He started seeing another girl in our class, so I threw the plastic ring in his face on the playground and never looked back."

Peter chuckled. "His loss."

"I like to think so."

He polished off the last of his beer. "Are your parents together?"

"At our age, you first need to ask if they're still alive," she teased. "They are and they are."

He whistled. "Sounds like they won the gold medal of marriages."

"They're very happy together," Rebecca said. "Always have been."

"You're a lucky woman."

Rebecca said nothing. She had her own thoughts on the subject, but she felt that some thoughts were best kept quiet, especially on a first date.

*My mom would've liked her.*

"Tell me about your mom," she said. "You said she was a cat magnet."

"I think the food was the magnet. She was just the hand that held it, but yeah." His expression grew soft and dreamy. "The strays seemed to know which house to go to."

"Your sister doesn't seem to share your sentimentality."

"No, she's a dog person. I forgive her for it," he said, injecting a teasing note into his voice.

"I have them both, so I can't pretend to have a favorite."

"But if you did it would obviously be cats," he said.

Tanya arrived with their fish tacos and a cheerful smile.

Rebecca stared at the plate in front of her and suddenly regretted choosing the tacos. How was she supposed to eat this without making a complete mess? She was going to embarrass herself.

*This was probably a bad choice. I'm going to have guacamole sliding down my arm.*

Rebecca stifled a laugh. At least they were on the same page.

"Would it be wrong to request a bib?" she asked.

"You too, huh?" He deftly lifted a taco to his mouth and took a bite without spilling any.

"Show-off," she said.

"I bet you can do it," he said. "Go on. I'll watch."

"No pressure then." She brought the taco to her mouth and tried to bite the end. She felt like a shark rising out of the water and opening its powerful jaws.

*Grace never would've eaten tacos in a restaurant. She would've considered it unladylike.*

Rebecca couldn't tell whether that was a plus or a minus. She chewed carefully, careful not to lose any pieces.

Tanya stopped by the table. "How is everything? Can I get you another drink?"

"One beer is good for me. I'll have water though." *My father might not have been able to stop at one beer, but I've got no problem with discipline.*

"Iced tea with lemon, please," Rebecca said.

"Feel free to have another," he said. "I'm the one driving."

"No, one is fine for me." She patted her stomach. "I'm saving room for dessert. I saw key lime pie on the menu."

"That's your favorite, huh?"

She nodded. "If it's on the menu, that's what I get."

"Mine is creme brûlée."

"Nice. I like that too." She paused. "But key lime pie is far superior."

She couldn't believe how easy it was to talk to him. Their conversation flowed and she acknowledged a spark that had been missing on her date with Tony. There'd been nothing wrong with her. He simply hadn't felt the spark—and truth be told neither had she. It was only sitting across from Peter now that she saw the situation clearly.

"I'm glad you weren't put off by the fact that I have cats," he said. "Some women think it's strange, like men can only like dogs or have some weird exotic pet like an albino alligator." He finished his last taco. "I have an affinity for cats though. My mom was their pied piper, and I was their human sibling."

"It probably stems from being the child of an alcoholic. You related to their struggle for survival." Rebecca quickly realized her mistake, but it was too late to snatch back the words. She could read minds; she couldn't erase them.

His eyes narrowed. "How do you know about that?"

Rebecca squirmed in her chair. "I…just assumed."

He leaned back against his chair and assessed her. "You assumed? That's a pretty accurate reading of someone you just met."

Rebecca's throat tightened. There was no way she could come clean. Somehow telling him she was a telepathic witch sounded much worse than admitting she was nosy.

He peered at her in disbelief. "Were you digging up info on me? Because I know my sister didn't tell you that. She tends to overshare, but she doesn't talk to anyone about our dad."

Silently, Rebecca debated her options. There was no easy way out of the situation, so she opted for the path of least weirdness. "A single woman can't be too careful these days," she finally said. "I asked a friend of mine to research you. I only wanted to make sure you weren't hiding a shady past or an arrest record."

His jaw hardened. "You could start by asking me instead of the internet." He tossed his napkin on the table. "If you must know, I've never been arrested, although I fought a guy in a bar once and he threatened to press charges. My lowest grade in school was a C and that was in gym class because I refused to pull my hair into a ponytail."

Rebecca sat perfectly still as a breeze whipped past them. "I'm sorry," she whispered.

He tugged his wallet from the pocket of his jeans and placed a handful of bills on the table. "I think we should call it a night. Thank you for a pleasant dinner." He pulled out his phone.

"Who are you calling?"

"A car service to pick you up because I'm not going to leave you stranded here," he said. "I use Ernie's Taxi Service, but I guess you already knew that from your research." He gave them the address and Rebecca's name. "Good luck with your fundraiser. I hope it all works out."

He stalked away from the table. Rebecca stared after him, uncertain what to do next. She'd expected to be rejected, of course, but not in such a grand fashion.

Tanya returned to the table, oblivious to Peter's exit. "Would you like to order dessert now or wait until your friend gets back from the restroom?"

"Just the check, please," she said in a small voice. "He isn't coming back."

## CHAPTER THIRTEEN

Rebecca tried her best to calm her nerves. The Memorial Day fundraiser started in less than an hour and she found herself in the middle of Julie's kitchen staring blankly at the wall. Fear seemed to have frozen her.

"Earth to Rebecca." Kate nudged her with an elbow. "Everything okay in there?"

"You're not still thinking about what you could've done differently on your date, are you?" Libbie asked.

Rebecca floated back to earth. "No, I've put it out of my mind." Okay, that was a lie, but she'd agreed to put it out of her mind for the day. "I'm just anxious about the fundraiser."

"I don't blame you," Libbie said, removing a tray of hors d'oeuvres from the oven. "This is a big deal."

"You're not supposed to say that," Julie accused. "You're supposed to say it's not a big deal and everything will work out for the best."

Libbie cringed. "Right. What she said."

Rebecca rubbed her temples. "What if I can't silence the voices? We're going to have so many people in one place. What if it gets to be too much?"

"Was it too much at The Cove?" Kate asked.

"No, but I was focused on Peter. It felt like we were the only two people in the world."

"God, I love that feeling," Libbie said.

"It was perfect until my telepathy ruined it." She folded her arms. "I want to find a spell that puts a stop to it."

Her three friends stared at her, unblinking.

"The date was that bad?" Julie asked.

"It was awful. I can't live like this. The voices are too much."

"He was a jerk to walk out," Kate said.

"No, he wasn't," Julie countered. "She hit a hot-button personal issue that she had no reason to know. I'm sure it triggered him."

"I felt terrible. There was so much pain on his face." Rebecca shook her head, trying to erase his expression from her memories. "I don't want anything like that to happen again."

"I still think he overreacted," Kate said.

"I don't think so," Rebecca countered. "Put yourself in his shoes. A woman you barely know seems to know more about you than what you've told her. Not just superficial information, but the kind you don't even acknowledge to your own family. It's creepy and suspicious."

"Women can't be too careful. We have to do our background checks," Libbie said. "Especially when we haven't met them through a mutual friend."

Rebecca sighed. "That's what I told him to cover my tracks." She'd never forget the expression on Peter's face. He'd looked stricken. "I don't think his response was unreasonable. If you could've heard his thoughts…" She gave an adamant shake of her head. "It doesn't matter. I don't have time to devote to dating right now anyway. The shelter is my priority. I should've said no to the date in the first place."

"You seem very focused on his needs," Kate said. "What about yours? Two people go on a date, just like two people are in a relationship. One isn't more important than the other."

"Maybe not, but try to see it from his perspective," Rebecca countered.

"You've been focused on taking care of those animals for so long, I think you've forgotten how to take care of yourself," Kate said.

Rebecca let the words sink in. Had she ever known how to put her needs first? She wasn't sure.

*How could she not want her gift?*

*I think she's the one overreacting.*

Rebecca squeezed her eyes shut, suddenly feeling overwhelmed by her friends' thoughts. "What if I can't get through this?"

Julie placed a reassuring hand on her shoulder. "If the voices are too much, then you go hide in a closet upstairs and shut the door until you feel comfortable. Believe me, those closets are soundproof. I've tested them."

Rebecca didn't have to ask to know what she meant. Julie had endured some challenging times in this house—first, caring for Greg before his death and then caring for her difficult mother until hers. Rebecca had no doubt that Julie found a few hiding places that helped her retain her sanity.

"You're going to be fine today," Kate said firmly. "This is your event and you are in complete command of your skills."

Behind her, Libbie bit back a smile. "I'm not so sure that Rebecca shares your confidence."

"Seriously," Julie chimed in. "She's been telepathic for what? A week? She's entitled to feel nervous."

Kate smoothed the front of her dress. "Fine. But I think nerves are a wasted emotion."

Libbie signaled to her children, who were acting as

members of her staff today. Usually they'd be working their own jobs, but Libbie had commandeered them for this special event, for which Rebecca was grateful.

"Kids, how are we doing with the displays for the silent auction?" Libbie asked.

Josh gestured to the table that had been set up in the family room. With its high ceilings and sunlit windows, it was the perfect place to showcase the offerings.

"All ready," he said.

"We should've included photos of the animals," Rebecca lamented.

"Not for an event like this," Kate said. "I think it's best to keep it simple. Most of the silent auction pieces have nothing to do with animals."

Rebecca knew she was probably starting to overthink everything—a sign that her nerves were getting the better of her.

*I hope this ends on time. I'm supposed to meet Darcy at her house. Her parents will only be gone until around eight, so we don't have a lot of time.*

Rebecca's ears perked up. She glanced at Josh, who was oblivious to her gift. She wasn't surprised he was thinking about sex. She wondered whether Libbie knew and if they'd had the talk. She was grateful when guests started to arrive. Hearing her date's thoughts was bad enough; she didn't want to know what teenage boys were thinking—not in any great detail.

Once the event started, Rebecca circulated outside, making sure to thank every single person for attending and tell them how much the shelter appreciated their generosity. The weather was on her side today, with a cloudless sky and a temperature in the low 70s with low humidity.

"Thank you so much for coming, Mrs. Bates," Rebecca said.

"We wouldn't miss an opportunity like this," the older woman said. "Myron and I go out of our way for pet charities, don't we, sweetheart?" She raised her voice at the end so Myron could hear her.

Unfortunately Myron seemed too buzzed on beer to respond coherently. After he'd bid on the Phillies tickets, he'd settled into an Adirondack chair by the lake and slipped into a world of his own until his burger was ready.

"We've raised a dozen animals in our life together," Mrs. Bates continued. "We even had horses and goats at one stage, but it got to be too much work for us once the kids were out of the house." *I miss that time. I think I was happiest in the midst of all that chaos. Ballet lessons and horseback riding and collecting eggs from the chickens.*

Rebecca gave her a sympathetic smile. "I bet it was great for the kids to grow up in that environment."

Mrs. Bates's eyes flickered with relief and Rebecca realized that she wanted to talk more about it. "It seemed like a world of insanity at the time, but I see now that I thrived in it. I don't do well in a quiet house and Myron is a wonderful husband, but he's a quiet man, which has its pros and cons, as you can imagine."

"You'd be welcome to volunteer at the shelter if you find yourself in need of noise," Rebecca said, only half joking. "We can always use another pair of experienced hands."

Mrs. Bates blinked rapidly. "I'm surprised I never thought of that. You're right. I think I'd quite enjoy it."

Rebecca tugged a business card from her pocket and handed it to her. "Call me and we'll set something up." Part of her wondered whether she should wait until the fate of the shelter had been decided, but she'd be nuts to let a potential volunteer slip away. Good volunteers were like gold.

While the guests feasted on Libbie's Kobe beef burgers and chilled wine, Rebecca gave her spiel about the shelter and rattled off the list of silent auction items. Aside from the tickets to sporting events, there was a fully catered dinner for six courtesy of Libbie. Julie's B&B room. Kate donated six life-coaching sessions and Rebecca donated six sessions of behavioral training for dogs. She could hear the guests' excited thoughts, hoping and wondering whether they'd win and calculating their bids.

"This is going really well," Kate said, bumping Rebecca's hip as she waited in line at the salad bar.

"People are going nuts over the sports tickets. Tell Lucas thank you for me."

"He was happy to do it."

"What's he doing with the kids today?" Rebecca asked.

"Took them on the boat. He texted earlier to complain it's busy out there, but it's Memorial Day—what did he expect?"

Rebecca made a point of checking in to make sure anyone who wanted to place a bid was able to do so.

"What did you bid on, Mr. Sawyer?" Rebecca asked.

Mr. Sawyer appeared to be around sixty-five. He wore a short-sleeved, collared top with a tiny logo on the chest and neatly pressed khakis.

"I've tried for the Flyers tickets and the Eagles, of course. My sons are huge fans." *I'll be disappointed if I don't win. I think this would be the best way to get them to spend time with me. They're always so busy.*

Rebecca felt a pang of sympathy for him. She knew from Julie he was a widower, so his kids were all he had.

"You should try for the B&B," she said. "If you win, maybe you could persuade your sons to come for a visit. They might enjoy lakeside accommodation."

Mr. Sawyer brightened. "That's not a bad idea. I saw kayaks on the beach out there and they love to kayak." He held up a finger. "Let me go put my bid in now before it's too late."

By the time the event concluded, Rebecca was ready to drop where she stood. She wasn't an introvert, but she'd done enough peopling for the next month. Rebecca felt drained from not only the interactions, but trying to keep the voices at bay. The hangover cure only seemed to stretch so far. She'd expended a lot of mental energy protecting herself from their thoughts. She hoped it wouldn't always be this exhausting.

Once the final guest vacated the premises and Josh and Courtney had been collected by their dad, the four friends sat outside in the Adirondack chairs with drinks in hand.

"Now that's how you do a fundraiser," Kate said, satisfied.

"How much did we raise?" Libbie asked.

Rebecca was already calculating the numbers on her phone. "Don't get me wrong, it's a good chunk of change, but it's not enough to buy the building." Not that she expected a mountain of cash to drop in her lap at the end of the night. This wasn't Cinderella and there was no fairy godmother.

Julie sipped her glass of wine. "What's your next move?"

Rebecca drew her knees to her chest. "Cry muffled sobs into my pillow? I don't know. I spoke to someone at Jump! about a fundraiser there, but they're booked up until August."

"We'll have to come up with another idea," Libbie said. She turned toward Kate. "Let us know when you think of one."

They laughed.

"I'll think tomorrow," Kate said, throwing a hand across her brow. "I'm spent."

"I'll only be able to think tomorrow until noon. That's when my parents are due to arrive," Rebecca said.

Libbie stood and stretched. "Not the best timing."

"No, but they so rarely visit. I'm hardly going to object."

"It's getting late. I should get going." Libbie collected

empty glasses from the other women and started toward the house.

Rebecca hopped to her feet. "Can I talk to you a quick second before you go?"

"Sure. What's up?"

She waited until they were out of earshot from the other women. "I hate to bring this up, but have you had the talk with Josh? It sounds like he and his girlfriend might be getting serious."

Libbie seemed taken aback. "He said that?"

"He was thinking about it. Well, thinking about going to her house because her parents would be out."

Libbie's cheeks reddened. "I mean, we've talked and I asked him to be safe and all that…" She sighed. "I'll have to ask Nick if they've touched on the topic again recently. Thanks for the tip."

Rebecca eyed her. "You're not mad?"

"Why would I be mad? I know you can't help what you overhear. I'm glad you told me."

Rebecca felt awash with relief. Her experience with Peter had been bad enough; she didn't want to have issues with her friends too.

"Thanks for everything today," Rebecca said. "You're the best."

Rebecca wasn't sure what she'd done to deserve three such amazing women in her life. It seemed incredible that one small act of kindness on her part had brought her to this point. A faint smile touched her lips as she remembered her chance encounter with Inga. The elderly woman had dropped her wallet during a walk in the park. Rebecca had been trailing behind her, walking the dogs, and had found the wallet on the ground. Inga had made it back to her car by the time Rebecca identified the wallet's owner, so Rebecca had to run huffing and puffing with two dogs in tow to reach the parking lot before she drove away.

Halfway there, Sugar decided she'd had enough and refused to move. Rebecca didn't make it. She watched the back of the car disappear around the bend. Thankfully she had the wallet which included the woman's license with her address, so Rebecca had ushered the dogs into the car and driven to Inga's house with the wallet.

"Oh, my," Inga had said, when Rebecca appeared on her doorstep with the wallet. "How did you get that?"

"I'm a pickpocket," Rebecca had joked and then realized it probably wasn't a good idea to joke about robbing an old woman. "I found it in the park."

Inga had smiled. "So you did. And it seems you went above and beyond to return it to me."

"Not really. I mean, you live locally. It wasn't a big deal."

"Don't minimize kindness. There isn't enough of it as it is." The older woman had regarded her carefully. "The name's Inga Paulsen, but I guess you know that already."

"Rebecca Angelos."

Inga had folded her arms and leaned her bony shoulder against the doorjamb. "Tell me, Rebecca Angelos. How do you feel about tequila?"

# CHAPTER FOURTEEN

Vincent and Gayle Angelos stood on the doorstep with a single suitcase in tow. It was small enough to store in the overhead compartment on an airplane.

"Do you need me to carry in a bag from the car?" Rebecca asked.

"No, we brought everything," her father said. His hair looked a bit thinner and whiter, and her mother had added a few more lines to her brow and around her mouth. They'd aged since she last saw them at Christmas.

She stepped aside to give them room to pass. Her mother gave the interior a cursory glance. "You've locked the animals away?"

"The dogs have been sequestered. The cats are roaming around here somewhere."

Her mother didn't move in for a hug, so Rebecca left it alone. "Are you thirsty? I have iced tea."

"Just water," her mother said.

"I'll take an iced tea," her father said. "Driving is thirsty work."

Rebecca smiled and went to the refrigerator for the jug.

She'd steeped the bags herself to get the right shade of brown she knew her parents liked.

*My arthritis is acting up. I should call Dr. Sherman.*

*Barb texted to say she booked us a weekend in the Hamptons for wine tasting. I didn't even know they had vineyards there.*

It didn't surprise her to learn she wasn't present in her parents' thoughts. Out of sight, out of mind and, apparently, in sight, out of mind too.

"How's everything at the shelter?" her father asked, once she delivered the drinks to the living room.

"Honestly, we're in a bit of a jam right now, but I'm working to fix it." She didn't tell them about the sale of the building, although she briefly mentioned her recent fundraising efforts. Rebecca knew better than to rely on her parents for any kind of help. They'd never been invested in her life; they weren't about to start now.

"Sounds like you've been busy," her mother said.

"You should hire more help," her father added. "You do too much as it is."

Angelica pranced into the room and walked straight past Rebecca to jump onto the section of the sofa between her parents. If she didn't know any better, Rebecca would've sworn the cat chose that spot on purpose, knowing it would irritate her mother.

Sure enough, Rebecca's mother leaned away. "Oh, I see the cat has made an appearance. I can feel a sneeze coming on."

"You're not allergic, Mom."

"No, but the hair still tickles my nose."

Her mother refused to admit she disliked cats. It was almost comical to watch.

"Where's that old cat that's afraid of everyone?" her father asked.

"Nico is under the bed, as expected." The Nebelung fled at

the first sign of visitors and would likely remain under the bed for the duration of their stay, only emerging to eat and use the litter box. "I'm a little jealous, to be honest. Bed sounds pretty good right now."

"You do seem tired," her mother said. "Is everything okay?"

"Work is stressful," she said.

*She works too hard*, her father thought. *And for peanuts. It's not worth it.*

He was wrong about that part. It was definitely worth it. Her father hadn't enjoyed his job teaching statistics at the local community college, so he didn't understand the satisfaction that came with loving your work no matter how time-consuming or stressful.

"How would you feel about moving this little party outdoors?" Rebecca asked.

Wordlessly her parents vacated the sofa and headed to the patio that overlooked the gorge. Rebecca suspected her mother was relieved to escape Angelica's close proximity.

"Beautiful part of the country here," her mother said, gazing at the view. "I like to check the weather app and see what's happening here. I'm surprised how different the weather can be when we don't really live that far apart."

"It's because we're in the mountains," Rebecca said.

Her father shook his head. "She checks the weather app like it's going to give her directions to the lost city of Atlantis."

Her mother looked at him, affronted. "So what? It's my favorite app."

Her father chuckled, clearly enjoying the good-natured torment of his wife. "She also loves to change the font on her emails. I keep telling her it's not an art project."

"Oh, I've noticed," Rebecca said. She'd received dozens of emails from her mother in comic sans and garamond, warning her about the latest internet scams and computer viruses. Her father sent jokes.

"Either way," her mother said, "you're very fortunate to have found this place, Rebecca. It's such a nice little nook in the world and the lake is wonderful."

*I think this place is fortunate to have found her*, her father thought.

Rebecca shot him a quizzical glance but said nothing. Did she really hear what she thought she heard? Compliments weren't exactly free-flowing in the Angelos house.

Angelica followed them outside and settled at Rebecca's feet, stretching her lithe body in the sunlight.

"She's a pretty cat, isn't she?" her mother said. That was likely the closest she'd warm to the cat.

Rebecca reached down to pet Angelica and hoped she didn't tweak her back in the process. You knew you'd reached middle age when the simple act of bending forward carried a level of risk. "Angelica lived with my friend before she died and Inga left her to me in her will." Among other treasures.

Her mother sniffed. "Naturally. She'd be a fool to leave an animal with anyone else."

Rebecca didn't feel the need to tell her about the other three cats. She'd take all the compliments she could get.

"I remember you mentioning Inga before," her father said. "Sounds like a fascinating woman."

"Oh, she was," Rebecca said. "I wish I'd had more time with her so I could've heard all her stories before she died. Each one was better than the last."

"Nonny was like that," her father said.

Nonny was his mother who'd arrived on a boat from Italy at the tender age of eighteen and made her own life here. She'd suffered several hardships, including the death of Lorenzo, her first husband and Rebecca's grandfather. She'd worked two jobs until she met and married her second husband and went on to have three more children. Nonny had probably been too busy trying to survive to provide Vincent Angelos with the love and attention he'd needed as a child.

Huh. Rebecca had spent so much time resenting her own lack of attention from her parents that she hadn't bothered to consider that he'd learned it as a part of his own upbringing. As far as he was concerned, it was a normal parent-child relationship.

Rebecca looked at her father with a fresh pair of eyes. "I'd love to know more about Nonny," she said.

Her father chuckled. "How much time do you have?"

Studying her father's deeply lined face, it occurred to Rebecca that her parents weren't getting any younger. As with Inga, if she didn't hear these stories now, she might never get the chance. The thought saddened her.

"What was that story about the crate of watermelons she used to tell?" Rebecca prodded.

Her father swallowed his iced tea and smacked his lips. "That is a classic Nonny story."

He launched into the story, quickly followed by another, and Rebecca lost herself in Nonny's adventures and mishaps. She was basically the Italian version of Lucille Ball. Thank goodness her father's memory was still so sharp. She knew there was no guarantee it would stay that way until he passed.

By the time he finished, the sun had started its descent and Rebecca's stomach was grumbling for food. "Should we order dinner or do you want to go somewhere?" she asked.

"Whatever works best for you," her mother said. *I've been dying for soft shell crab.*

"I'm in the mood for seafood," Rebecca said. "Anybody else?"

Her mother perked up. "It's like you read my mind."

The sound of a car in the driveway startled Rebecca and she nearly spilled the bowl of water she was in the process of refilling. Her parents were long in bed and Rebecca wasn't expecting anyone at this late hour. She dragged herself to the window to see Peter Putnam's truck. What was he doing here?

She opened the front door before he had a chance to knock or ring the bell. The sound would send all the animals into a frenzy and wake up her parents.

She opened the door a crack, holding back the curious animals with her leg. "Hi. You're the last person I expected to see on my doorstep tonight."

With a sheepish grin, Peter held up a transparent container that housed a generous slice of key lime pie. "I'm here to apologize for my behavior. I'm sure you're going to think I'm full of it, but leaving you at the restaurant like that…It's not who I am. I hope you'll accept this peace offering."

She took the container. "I'm not foolish enough to turn down key lime pie."

"Would it be okay if I came in for a minute? I promise I won't stay long. I'd like to explain myself and it's a conversation better had in person." *Please say yes.*

"Just give me one second and I'll put the dogs away." She didn't want to make the conversation any more difficult for Peter than it already was. Having unfamiliar dogs trying to lick him the whole time wasn't the distraction he needed.

Once she'd sequestered the dogs, she returned to the door to let him in. "How about a drink? You seem like you could use one."

He offered a half smile. "Do I seem that out of sorts?"

"Not really," she said. "It would just be an excuse for me to have one too."

He laughed. "In that case, I'd love one."

She guided him to the kitchen where she opened the liquor cabinet. He peered over her shoulder. "Wow, that's quite an extensive selection."

She craned her neck to look at him. "Before you get any ideas about what kind of lush I am, I'm a member of a cocktail club, so I have a lot of ingredients on hand."

He squinted at her. "Not really doing much to dispel the lush idea."

Now it was her turn to laugh. "How about we keep it simple with a glass of wine? Or I have beer in the fridge. My parents are visiting so I bought beer for my dad."

"A beer works for me." He leaned his back against the counter. "Your parents are here? Are you sure this isn't a bad time?"

"They're asleep," she said. "It's way past their bedtime."

He chuckled. "I look forward to the day when nine o'clock is past my bedtime."

Rebecca poured a glass of beer for him and a glass of red wine for herself. "If you don't mind leaving covered in animal hair, you're welcome to sit on the sofa."

"You seem to have forgotten that I have two cats of my own."

At the mention of cats, Angelica came trotting in to greet them. She walked straight over to Peter and rubbed her back against his leg.

"Hello, beautiful." He bent down to pet her.

Rebecca glanced at the patio. "What's the temperature like? Would you rather sit outside?"

He resumed an upright position. "Always."

They settled on the chairs outside and Rebecca tipped her

head back to admire the visible constellations. She loved a clear night.

"I don't want to overstay my welcome, so I'll get right to the point," Peter said. "I owe you an explanation for my behavior." He took another drink from the glass. "I mentioned my ex-wife, but I didn't really get into the details of our marriage because…Well, mostly because I don't think it's appropriate for a first date and I don't like to speak poorly of her. She's not a bad person. It's just that she did things during the marriage that didn't sit well with me and I suddenly had this sense of déjà vu when you seemed to know things about me that you shouldn't."

"About that…" Rebecca still hadn't decided how much to share. The truth seemed too strange, yet Ethan knew about Libbie's gift and Lucas knew about Kate's, and they seemed to have no problem accepting their magic.

"Let me get through this first, if you don't mind," Peter said, "or I might not be able to manage it. Kind of hard for me to talk about my feelings, but it's something I've been working on."

Rebecca sat back against the chair and listened.

"My ex-wife was controlling. She used to snoop in my phone and read all my messages and emails. In my defense, I'd never given her a reason not to trust me. Not once. There were no issues in the marriage of that kind. I recognize now that it was because of her own trust issues from childhood, but they wrecked our marriage. At the time, I didn't know how to deal with her behavior. I would get angry and frustrated. It took me years to realize that her behavior wasn't about me."

"But not in time to save the marriage," Rebecca said.

He shook his head. "I wasn't self-aware enough to see what was happening and in hindsight I see I didn't handle it well. I took everything as a personal attack, which it was, but it came from a place of hurt. Honestly, I don't think we would've worked out anyway. As far as I know, she hasn't taken steps to work on herself. I imagine whatever issues she brought into our marriage, she's continued to take into every relationship since then."

It stood to reason. Rebecca was impressed that he'd taken it upon himself to look inward and see whether his own actions had contributed to the demise of the relationship.

"I appreciate you telling me this," she said. "It helps me to understand your reaction a bit more. Ernie's a nice guy, by the way. Thinks the world of you." Although she hadn't been keen to hear it on the ride home from their date.

Angelica appeared and Rebecca expected the cat to join her. Instead, the cat swerved and jumped onto Peter's lap. A surprisingly good sign. Angelica was picky; the cat didn't warm to just anyone.

"Ernie's as reliable as a clock. I like people I can rely on."

Rebecca took a sip of her wine. She needed liquid courage right now. The sensible part of her said to keep her secret, but another part of her sensed that Peter was worth taking a leap of faith. She really liked him and if the relationship had any hope of continuing, she had to tell him the truth. If he was going to accept her, that meant accepting all of her, including her gift. If he rejected her, then she was no worse off than she already was. Whatever his response, she could handle it.

"There's something I should tell you and you're going to think I'm nuts."

He regarded her curiously. "There are a lot of interesting adjectives I would use to describe you, Rebecca, but nuts isn't one of them." *Gorgeous. Kind. Sexy. Compassionate. But not nuts.*

Rebecca's face grew flushed as the compliments rolled through his mind. "Hold that thought, literally. Now is probably a good time to tell you that I'm telepathic."

Peter nearly spit out his beer. "Excuse me?"

"I'm telepathic. I can read minds." She paused. "I can read *your* mind."

Peter stared at her for what seemed like an eternity. Finally he said, "That's how you knew those things about me. I'd been thinking about them during our date."

Rebecca nodded. "I didn't mean to pry. I can't help it. It's still kind of new and I haven't learned how to control it. It comes and goes, although I've managed to dull it so it doesn't overwhelm me. I shouldn't have said anything about your dad. It slipped out."

He frowned. "You haven't been telepathic your whole life? This is a…midlife change?"

Rebecca laughed. "Along with a bunch of other changes, yes. It's a long story, but it all started with my friend Inga, the founder of the cocktail club I mentioned. She was a witch and when she died, she divided her magical assets between me and three of our friends."

Peter mouth dropped open. "A witch?"

She waved a hand. "I know what you're thinking. No, we don't have pointy black hats, although we do have cats."

"Do you dance under the moon naked?"

She suppressed a smile. "We have been known to skinny dip after a few bottles of wine."

"Now I'm kind of wishing I could read minds. I'd love to see what's in yours right now."

Rebecca felt a rush of warmth through her veins. Not only did Peter not seem freaked out, he seemed genuinely interested. She could hear a dozen curious thoughts spinning around in his mind.

He tipped his head back to admire the night sky. "This is, hands down, the most amazing news I've ever gotten after an apology."

"Do you find yourself apologizing often?" she teased. "Because that could be indicative of another problem."

He chuckled. "I knew you were special, Rebecca. I just didn't know *how* special."

"You believe me?"

He turned to look at her. "Of course I do. What reason could you possibly have for making up a story like that?"

She exhaled the breath she'd been holding. "Thank you."

He stared at her intently. "Thank you for your honesty. Trust is a big deal to me, as you can probably imagine."

They lapsed into normal conversation and Rebecca felt herself relaxing. She updated him on the fundraiser and the lack of suitable alternative locations.

"What about making a pet calendar featuring animals from the shelter?" he suggested. "I always buy the ones with photos from national parks, but I'd buy one with a bunch of cute animals."

Rebecca mulled it over. "Do people buy calendars anymore?"

"Sure. They like to hang them up at work so they have something nice to look at while they count down the hours until they can go home." He tipped back his glass to polish off the last of his beer. "Not that I have to worry about that. My office is my workshop right next to my house."

Now that she thought about it, she realized he was right. She still saw calendars when she went to places like the dentist and to see the accountant. She'd noticed one in Ethan's office too.

"That's a great idea, thanks." It would also be a way to put the animals front and center since the Memorial Day fundraiser didn't directly involve them.

"No problem. I wish I could do more. I hate that this guy has put you in such a tough situation."

"It isn't personal," she said, quoting Brian Shea. "It's only business."

"Yeah, but sometimes it's more important to look at the big picture. Sure, he's going to make money, but at what cost?" *Brian Shea sounds like a tool.*

Rebecca was enjoying their conversation so much that she was shocked to look at her phone and see that it was midnight.

"I should let you get to bed," Peter said. "It's much later than I thought it would be and you never even ate your pie."

"It's in the fridge," she said. "I'll have it tomorrow." She paused. "Or later today, I guess."

He stretched his legs out in front of him before rising to his feet. Watching him now inhabiting her safe space, Rebecca felt like she'd known him forever. It was a good feeling and she embraced it.

"Good night, Rebecca. Thank you for being such a lovely hostess." He leaned down and brushed his lips against hers. "I hope this means we can go out again soon."

"I'd like that," she said, smiling at him.

She walked him to the door and he kissed her one more time before exiting the house. Rebecca could hardly contain her excitement. She'd told him the truth and he hadn't run screaming from the house. He hadn't rejected her. More importantly, his thoughts seemed to correspond to his actions. He wasn't saying one thing but thinking another. Peter Putnam was exactly the man he appeared to be.

## CHAPTER FIFTEEN

Rebecca was grateful that the entire Bernstein family was volunteering today. She needed the extra help if she expected to get the animals bathed and groomed before the photo shoot. It helped that Charlotte Bernstein was an organizational wiz. She would've loved to spread out the baths, but if she left too much time in between, the animals would cease to look their best by the time it was their turn for a closeup. It was like Rebecca's school photos. No matter how nicely she'd dressed and brushed her untamed hair on picture day, her time slot would inevitably fall after lunch and she'd show up on the stool with food stains on her dress and her hair in knots. The forced square smile never impressed anyone either. She was pretty sure her parents would buy them but not send them to relatives.

"I wish we could stay for the photo shoot and help you," Mrs. Bernstein said.

"I don't mind staying," Mr. Bernstein said.

His wife smacked him with a wet towel. "You're only saying that because it's my mother's birthday party."

He splayed his hands. "What? Rebecca needs help. It would be rude not to offer."

Mrs. Bernstein glared at her husband, but Rebecca could tell from her thoughts she wasn't truly angry.

"You said your parents are in town," Mr. Bernstein said. "Maybe they can drop by."

Rebecca snorted. "They're at the lake. Honestly, they'd be more of a hindrance than a help. They're not animal people."

"Then where did you come from?" Mrs. Bernstein asked.

"They had each other for companionship," Rebecca said, shrugging. "I needed my own."

Mrs. Bernstein rolled her eyes. "Hang out at our house. We've got companionship coming out the wazoo."

Rebecca laughed. "I'm all set, thanks. Anyway, Peaches will be here soon. I think we can handle it between the two of us."

Mr. Bernstein patted her arm. "I have faith in you. Put us down on the list for the calendar. We want to be your first sale."

"Absolutely," Rebecca promised.

Jack, the eldest Bernstein child, finished toweling off the final dog. "His fur takes forever to dry."

"It's fine," Rebecca said. "It'll look dry in the photos." She hoped. Images of wet dogs likely conjured up that wet dog smell, which was off-putting for many people.

Once the Bernsteins left, Rebecca set to work staging the photo shoot area. She threw a plain white blanket on the floor and made sure there was enough natural light coming through the window. She placed Oatmeal on the blanket to test the light through the lens of her camera phone. The cat was too lazy to make a run for it, so she was the ideal choice for this experiment.

"What do you think you're doing?"

Rebecca straightened and turned to look at Peaches. "What does it look like?"

Peaches clucked her tongue. "Boomers. Here, let me help you."

"I'm Gen-X, thank you very much."

"Never heard of it." Peaches plucked the phone from Rebecca's hand and opened the camera app. "No offense, but I probably have a lot more experience than you with this sort of thing."

Rebecca wanted to laugh at the idea of a twenty-year-old having more experience than Rebecca at anything, but Peaches was right. Kids today grew up with technology, whereas Rebecca had grown up with toys and sticks in the woods. She'd spend hours by the reservoir near her childhood home, skimming stones and searching for tadpoles. If it weren't for her hours wandering the neighborhood, she wasn't sure she would've developed her deep love of animals. The first stray she'd ever befriended was in the woods behind her house—a cat she'd named Scruffy because of his disheveled tail. Scruffy had been followed by Jewel and a dog named Basset that lived two doors down. Like Rebecca, Basset's family didn't pay him much attention and he ended up hanging out in the woods with Rebecca on weekends and after school. It was Rebecca, in fact, who'd discovered the tumor on Basset's leg and reported it to Mr. Milliken. Rebecca had been outraged when she later discovered the Milliken family wasn't seeking treatment. Her parents had explained that not every family could afford the level of medical care that cancer required—that even human families sometimes had to forgo the care they needed because of spiraling costs. It had been a hard lesson for Rebecca, one she hadn't taken well. Despite her attachment to the dog, she hadn't even been given the opportunity to say goodbye to Basset. The memory still gnawed at her bones. Animals like

Basset had saved her from a lonely childhood. Now the animals were the ones who needed saving and Rebecca refused to let them down.

"We need music," Peaches said. "It will add to the experience."

"Theirs or ours?"

"Why not both? Our experience matters too."

Rebecca gave a crisp nod. "Okay then. I'll put on my playlist." Rebecca knew that Peaches wasn't the type of young person to offer sarcastic commentary on Rebecca's musical taste.

Rebecca heard the beginning of *Baby Got Back* and danced her way back to the staging area.

"See?" Peaches said. "It's already more fun."

She was right; it was.

"Who's on the list for January?" Peaches asked.

"Jazz, Falcon, and Mogwai."

Peaches nodded. "That trio makes sense." She glanced at the setup in the corner of the room. "That's your background?"

Rebecca heard the note of disapproval in the girl's tone. "Not exciting enough?"

Peaches frowned at the blanket laden with toys. "Um, where is the winter wonderland? The backdrop should reflect the month. Have you never looked at a calendar?"

"Have you?"

Peaches moved a hand to her hip. "It just so happens I have a calendar on the wall in my bedroom."

"What's on it?"

"Unicorns."

Rebecca gave her an appraising look. "Yeah, that tracks. I've been so busy and this idea was sort of last minute…I didn't think through the details." She was desperate. She'd do a thousand last-minute events if it meant saving the shelter.

Peaches squeezed her shoulder. "Not to worry. I'm here to help. I was the star of my art classes." *Too bad my parents consider art nothing more than a hobby.*

Rebecca cut a sideways glance at her. "Why aren't you taking art classes at the college level?"

"My parents won't pay for it," she admitted. "That's why I'm working now instead of going to college. I want to save enough money to pay my own way."

"But you're only a volunteer here. You could be spending those hours earning money for school."

Peaches smiled. "My parents got me involved in community service from a young age. I chose animals as my passion project. My mom volunteers at the soup kitchen with my sister, and my dad and brother volunteer for the thrift store. I used to volunteer there too, until I found this place."

Rebecca wanted to hug her. "And I'm so glad you did." She paused. "For people who don't view art as a worthy pursuit, I'm surprised they picked the name Peaches."

She tossed a blonde braid over her shoulder. "Oh, my real name is Georgina. That's where Peaches came from. They used to call me their sweet Georgia peach when I was little and Peaches stuck."

"That's freakin' adorable."

Peaches motioned to the two cats curled together in the crate. "Not as adorable as those two." She opened the crate door and snapped a photo. "We should put up a bunch of candids on the shelter website too. People will love looking at them."

Rebecca recognized the beat of *It's Tricky* by Run-D.M.C. and laughed. "It's like my playlist knows what's happening right now."

"I don't know about your playlist, but the universe knows," Peaches said.

Rebecca observed her. "Anyone ever tell you that you're an old soul?"

Peaches wore a vague smile. "We're all old souls. Some of us just recognize it sooner than others."

"I need the ferrets now," Rebecca said.

Peaches smirked. "Let me guess. Ferret February?"

"I like alliteration. So sue me."

"Well, at least we only have Dino and Scooter," Peaches said. "That makes it easy." Dino and Scooter had come from the same home when a teenaged boy went off to college and had to leave his pets behind. His parents had no interest in continuing to care for them, so the duo ended up at the shelter. The ferrets got along well together, which made life easier for Rebecca.

"What about a Valentine theme for them?" Rebecca asked.

"Love is in the air," Peaches sang as she wandered across the room to retrieve the ferrets from their enclosure. "These two clearly adore each other."

The ferrets scampered away from the photo shoot and Rebecca spent the next twenty minutes chasing them.

"Don't film this!" she yelled as Peaches laughed, capturing all the hijinks on the phone.

"Why not? This is the best part. We'll laugh about it later."

"Much later," Rebecca grumbled. She was exhausted by the time they finished with the ferrets. Only nine months to go. She wanted to sink to the floor and weep.

"Are we doing shamrocks for March?" Peaches asked. "If so, I have a filter we can use for that."

Rebecca pursed her lips, thinking. "Do you think shamrocks are too played out?"

"What else do you suggest? Pints of Guinness?"

Rebecca laughed. "I think that would be adorable. Set up a little bar scene and have the dogs with beer." Her eyes popped. "March Madness. They can wear sports jerseys."

Peaches nodded her approval. "That would appeal to a certain crowd." She turned to face the enclosure. "Where are we going to get a bunch of tiny sports jerseys on short notice?"

Rebecca knew exactly where to call. The woman who owned a local children's clothing store had adopted two cats from the shelter and she knew for a fact that Lydia stocked a supply of jerseys for infants and toddlers.

"Let me make a call."

As Rebecca hoped, Lydia offered to donate six jerseys to the cause. She'd heard about the sale of the building and had tried to get tickets to the Memorial Day fundraiser.

"Definitely let me know when that calendar is out. I'll put up flyers in the store too," she'd said.

They got through April, May, and June before Peaches insisted they stop to eat. Rebecca would've kept going and then buried her face in a plate of pasta later if the volunteer hadn't saved her from that fate. Her mother texted during lunch to say they'd finished at the lake and were headed back to the house for a nap. Rebecca mustered enough energy to respond with a thumbs up emoji.

After their break, Rebecca paced in front of the enclosures. "Who do you like for July?"

"What about Meatball and Elvis together?" Peaches asked.

Rebecca pictured the bulldog and the pug side by side. "I think we should put them with Tator Tot and Dexter."

Peaches lit up. "That's genius."

Tator Tot and Dexter were the two tallest, skinniest dogs at the shelter. They would look hilarious next to the two shortest, squattest dogs.

"They all need red, white, and blue bowties," Peaches said. "What about having them wear Uncle Sam hats?"

"I think the taller ones should wear the hats and the

shorter ones should wear the bowties. It will accentuate their differences."

Peaches wagged a finger. "See? And you think you're not creative. Where do we get these hats?"

"I saw them in the window of Toppers." Toppers was an eclectic store on the corner that changed its inventory to match the season. She raided the petty cash fund and sent Peaches on a quick mission to procure the hats and ties.

The dogs were incredibly cooperative all things considered, and they quickly moved on to August.

"Are we ready for the rabbits?" Rebecca asked.

Peaches observed the interior of the hutch. "I don't know. Bonny's in a mood."

"What's she doing? Lying on top of Frankie's food bowl so she can't eat?"

"You know them so well," Peaches said.

"Frankie must've done something to aggravate her."

"Right now she's using her head to dislodge Bonny's body so she can get to the bowl."

"Maybe we'll come back to them," Rebecca said. She didn't have time for divas during this photo shoot. "Let's do the beauty queens."

"I assume you mean Artemis and Bob."

Artemis was a gorgeous calico and Bob was a Persian and the two were inarguably the most beautiful cats in the shelter. Rebecca debated whether to bother to include them on the calendar. She knew from experience they'd likely be adopted before the calendar even made it to the printer.

"Do you think we should stick to the long-term residents?" Rebecca asked.

"I think we need a month that's all pit mixes," Peaches said.

"Brilliant," Rebecca agreed. "It's August so we should do a

summer theme with a beach ball and towels. Maybe a sun umbrella open behind them."

Peaches nodded, smiling. "So cute."

"I'll set that up now." Given that it was almost summer, she had easy access to everything she needed. "What should we do for September? Apple orchards? School supplies?"

Peaches stilled and Rebecca heard the thought before she said it out loud—

"Superheroes," Peaches declared. She pointed to the crate that housed Rango, the bearded dragon. "Rango can wear his Batman cape."

Rebecca clamped a hand over her mouth. Superhero September. "Let's do it. I love it."

"We have to feature Sir Sebastian Barkalot or he'll make us regret it," Rebecca said.

Peaches contemplated the noisy Maltese. "I think we'll regret it either way."

Sir Sebastian was a sweetheart, but he definitely liked to be heard. Sometimes he was so loud and persistent, he managed to drown out the voices in Rebecca's head. She wasn't sure which she preferred.

"What if we include him in a month with all the cats?" Rebecca asked. "We can position him in the middle and put the cats all around him."

"I think his bark will scare the cats away."

"That's why you're here," Rebecca said. "You can play cat herder." She snapped her fingers. "He can be Santa and the cats can be elves. We'll put wrapped presents around them. The cats will love the boxes and bows."

Peaches brightened. "I can get my sister to bring wrapped boxes. We use them as decorations on the front porch at Christmastime. I'll text her right now."

"You took an awful lot of videos on my phone," Rebecca said, staring at the camera app.

Peaches snatched the phone from her. "And don't you dare delete them. They're hilarious."

"Yes, but are you laughing with us or at us?"

Peaches shrugged. "Who cares what anyone thinks? You're having fun and it's all for a good cause."

Rebecca could learn a lot from twenty-year-old Peaches.

They'd just finished November when Ginny arrived, her arms laden with empty decorative boxes and Santa hats.

"Can I stay and help?" Ginny asked, once she saw what they were doing.

"Absolutely," Rebecca said. "We could use the extra hands."

Ginny set up the display while Rebecca and Peaches got the animals ready. They changed the background music to Christmas carols and each took turns dancing with the animals.

Rebecca had no idea whether they'd sell enough calendars to make a dent in their goal, but she had to admit they were having a grand time doing it. She wanted to believe it was the journey that mattered and not the destination, but in this case, it was definitely the destination. She had to find a way to raise the money the shelter needed, to prove that she could make a difference. Rebecca realized with a start how desperately she wanted to succeed, not only for the animals but for herself. She couldn't decide whether it was pathetic or perfectly normal. Instead of judging her feelings, she decided to work to better understand them. Inga once told her there was one question more important than any other. Rebecca had jokingly responded with who, what, where, when, and how?

"You missed the most important one," Inga had said.

"Who? No, I said that one already." Admittedly, Rebecca had been a little tipsy at the time.

Inga had flashed an enigmatic smile. "Why?"

## CHAPTER SIXTEEN

"How are your parents doing?" Julie asked.

Rebecca had her friend on speaker as she updated the inventory spreadsheet on the computer. "Fine. They're at the lake again."

"Did they rent a boat?"

Rebecca laughed. "Definitely not. I gave them two badges for the beach at the club. Mom had her Nora Roberts book in her tote bag and Dad had his latest sci-fi novel so they're set for the day."

"I bet they were horrified when you told them about the shelter."

"I'm sure they would be, but I didn't tell them." Although Rebecca didn't hear the gasp, she sensed there'd been one.

"Why didn't you tell them?"

"What's the point?" Rebecca asked. "There's nothing they can do." And they weren't interested in the details of her life. They preferred a broad overview so they could get straight back to their own lives.

"Still, they're your parents, they're visiting, and you're in the middle of a crisis."

Rebecca felt a knot forming in her stomach. "Did you confide in Doris about everything you were dealing with?" Rebecca knew the answer was no.

"That's unfair," Julie said. "You know I didn't have a great relationship with my mom when she was alive."

"Just because my mom isn't overly critical of me doesn't mean we have the kind of relationship that means sharing all my problems. It's a surface-level relationship and that's fine." It meant no drama. No fighting. No constant phone calls or guilt trips.

Rebecca was too focused on the spreadsheet to pick up Julie's thoughts, which was for the best as far as she was concerned. She didn't need telepathy to know what her friend was thinking right now.

"Maybe consider sharing the burden a little," Julie advised. "Your parents won't be around much longer and…"

"I hate to cut you off, but I really need to get this spreadsheet updated before the end of the day and I'm meeting my parents for dinner before cocktail club."

Julie didn't push back. "Okay, let me know if there's anything I can do. I was thinking I could host a casino night if you think it would help."

Rebecca closed her eyes and inhaled deeply. Julie was such a good friend who only wanted the best for Rebecca. "Thanks, Julie. That's a great idea. Why don't we talk about it later tonight?"

"Absolutely. I already have a few ideas."

They said their goodbyes and Rebecca cut a glance at Iago. "Don't look at me like that."

"No good," the parrot squawked.

The buzzer drew Rebecca's attention to the door. "Hold that thought, Iago," she said. *Please. Do not share any thoughts.* If Rebecca began overhearing the animals' thoughts on top of everyone else, she would officially lose her mind. As much as she loved animals, she had no interest in becoming Dr. Dolittle.

A man entered the shelter, early thirties, with sharp eyes and an engaging smile. He wore jeans and a T-shirt featuring a band Rebecca didn't recognize. She noticed dark mud caked on his boots.

"Hi, welcome to Cloverleaf Critters. I'm Rebecca."

"Bud. Nice to meet you, Rebecca. I was told this was the place to come for a forever friend."

Something about him set off alarm bells, although Rebecca couldn't see any outward signs of a problem. His mind seemed relatively blank at the moment, although she'd drank another hangover tea this morning to dull her telepathy. She picked out a few vague thoughts regarding a missing key and a mental note to power wash the patio. She would have to probe the old-fashioned way and see what she could uncover.

"What kind of friend are you looking for?" Rebecca asked.

"I'm a dog person myself." His gaze swept the room. "Seems like slim pickings out here. I guess you keep most of them in another room."

Rebecca maintained a neutral expression. "It's never slim pickings at a shelter."

Bud nodded at Iago. "Didn't expect to see that at a shelter. Thought you were all dogs and cats."

"*That* is Iago and he's a parrot." She watched him carefully. "Are you looking for an indoor or an outdoor dog?"

"Indoor," he said smoothly.

Her gaze dropped to his muddy boots. "Someone to take on long hikes maybe?"

"Sure," he said casually.

Rebecca was surprised none of his thoughts seemed to relate to the adoption of a dog, which only increased her suspicion. It was as though he didn't care which dog he took home.

"Have you ever taken care of a pet before, Bud?" she asked. She opened the crate and scooped out Elvis, who'd been keeping her company. "This is Elvis."

Bud shook the pug's paw. "Nice to meet you. He's cute, but I'm partial to bigger dogs. More manly, you know?" He winked. *I hear they pay more for the larger ones. No point going to all this trouble to bring them a little guy like this.*

Rebecca nuzzled the dog's face to hide her expression. She knew something was amiss. That explained why he seemed so disinterested. He genuinely didn't care about the dog, only that it would earn him money. Was it a dog fighting ring or something else?

"I have a few larger dogs in need of a good home. Maybe a Doberman?" she asked.

He didn't perk up at the mention of a Doberman, which likely ruled out a dog fighting ring. He also didn't ask specifically about pit bulls, another potential clue.

Bud scratched his scruffy chin. "I don't need a pure bred. Anything on the cheaper end of the scale suits me." He paused. "What I mean is I'd rather spend the money on the dog's care than on his fees."

"Our fees are the same for any dog. We're not breeders," she said.

He laughed awkwardly. "Right. Of course." He flashed that charming smile again. "See? This is what happens when you're a first-time pet owner. You need a lot of help."

"What made you decide to get a dog now?" she asked, adopting her friendliest tone so as not to arouse his suspicion.

"Girlfriend left me." He shrugged. "I figure I'd trade…" *One bitch for another.* "Figure I'd try a different sort of companionship. Mix things up a little. Dogs are loyal, right?"

Rebecca put Elvis safely back in the crate. "If you treat them well." Which she knew this man had no intention of doing. "Are you looking for a male or female?"

"Female," he said. "Women tend to like me better." There was that smile again, except Rebecca saw cruelty in his mouth now. The charm had all but evaporated.

"You'll have to let me in on your secret," she said. "I'm forty-seven and I still haven't figured them out."

*They're all the same, lady. Just tell 'em they're pretty and they'll eat out of your hand.*

Rebecca fought the urge to kick this guy in the crotch. Did he want to breed puppies? "I have a few females that might appeal to you. They're all spayed and up to date on shots." She listened intently to his thoughts to see if spaying was an issue.

*Don't think the lab cares if they're spayed. They just said they prefer to test on females.*

Rage washed over her. Her body was Bruce Banner, but her anger was Hulk-sized. She wanted to leap across the counter and throttle his turkey neck. Still, she had to contain her emotions. If she made it obvious she knew what his real intentions were, he'd simply move on to another shelter. Rebecca didn't just want to prevent him from selling one of *her* dogs to a heartless laboratory for testing; she wanted to prevent him from selling *any* dog. That meant biting her tongue and biding her time.

"You know what?" she said. "I have an important meeting to get to, but if you leave me your name and number, I'll give you a call and we can arrange a good time for you to come back. I wouldn't want to rush you into a decision before you're ready."

Bud's thoughts were filled with disappointment, but he didn't show it. Rebecca handed him a scrap of paper and a pen and he jotted down his information.

"I didn't realize you had such limited hours," he said, a passive-aggressive admonishment.

"We're on a tight budget these days. I had to let my full-time staff member go recently."

"That's too bad." *What a waste of time.*

"It is, but we've increased our fundraising efforts."

"Sounds good." He saluted her. "See you soon, I guess."

*Not if I can help it*, she thought.

She was relieved when the door closed behind him. She'd let the local police know about him as soon as he drove away. She would've liked to learn more about the lab, but she'd take what she could get. Maybe the police could extract that information from him. What a scumbag.

"Good work," Iago squawked.

She jerked toward the parrot, startled. "What?"

"Good work," the parrot repeated.

Rebecca smiled at him. "Thanks. It really was good work, wasn't it?"


Rebecca parked in Kate's driveway with a bottle of tequila on the seat beside her because it was that kind of night. Inga had been a proponent of tequila shots and her friends were more than happy to continue that tradition.

Before Rebecca could open the car door, her phone buzzed and MaryAnn's name stared back at her. She swiped the phone to her ear. "Hi. Any good news?"

"No new listings, I'm afraid," MaryAnn reported. "I've contacted everyone I know and asked them to call me the second they know of anything."

Rebecca tried to disguise her disappointment. "Thanks. I'm not expecting a miracle." *Just hoping for one.*

"I hate to sound negative, but I know there's another no-kill shelter about fifty minutes from here. They can't take all of yours, of course, but I'm sure they'd be able to handle a few."

Rebecca pinched the bridge of her nose to keep herself from crying. "Thanks, MaryAnn. I'll start looking into alternate arrangements tomorrow." She'd been putting off the inevitable, but MaryAnn was right; it was time to start contacting other shelters.

Cat-Cat greeted Rebecca at the door and she took a moment to rub the cat's slender body. "You're living your best life here, aren't you?"

The cat purred in response. Kate had been uncertain about caring for the cat at first, but Rebecca could tell from the cat's disposition they'd gotten over any bumps in the road.

The friends congregated in Kate's kitchen while the blender whirred with their mango margaritas. She poured four glasses and they toasted to Inga, followed by their compliment circle.

"Is anyone else thrilled that the good weather is finally here?" Libbie asked, slipping off her shoes. "I feel like this past winter was particularly brutal."

"Imagine how people must've felt in olden days," Julie said. "We think we're strong, but those women must've been incredible."

"Childbirth would've killed me," Libbie said.

"One of yours had an enormous head, didn't they?" Kate prodded.

"Yes, but that's not what I mean," Libbie replied. "The lack of drugs would've done me in. No drugs? No thanks."

"I would've died from malnourishment," Rebecca said. "Those women couldn't get takeout from Nino's."

"I drink a lot of water," Kate said. "I think I would've died of dysentery."

Rebecca stretched her arms over her head, finally

allowing herself to relax. "I'm so glad we live in this century. I would've been terrible in any other one. Imagine having no rights as a woman."

Kate scrunched her nose. "Imagine your father arranging your marriage like you're a piece of his property. Bargaining your life away like you're a prized pig." She flicked a sleepy glance at Rebecca. "No offense to pigs."

Snorting in response, Rebecca realized the alcohol had finally kicked in.

"Has anyone ever brought a pig to the shelter?" Libbie asked.

Rebecca mulled it over. "No, but we once had a swan. She wasn't very nice either. Bit Ida's finger."

Kate frowned at her. "Who on earth unloaded a swan at the shelter?"

"We don't know. Ida was in the back and someone buzzed and ran," Rebecca said. "Thankfully we found a new home for her. Some estate on the Main Line wanted a swan for its reflection pond."

The other women laughed.

"My reflection pond is called the bathtub," Julie said.

"Says the woman with the best view of the lake," Rebecca pointed out.

"But I don't own the lake," Julie shot back. "Besides, Kate's view of the lake is pretty nice too."

Simultaneously they turned their gazes to the water outside.

"We're very lucky," Libbie said quietly.

The other women murmured their assent.

"Inga would've liked this," Kate said.

"The view?" Julie asked.

Kate shook her head. "No, seeing us carry on with the cocktail club."

"She was an inspirational lady," Libbie said.

"Life changing," Julie agreed.

Kate turned to look at Julie. "Have you seen any ghosts this week?"

"One," Julie said. "An old woman who lived at the retirement village. She wanted me to tell her neighbor that it was her dog that got the other one's dog pregnant. She hadn't wanted to confess when she was still alive because she was too embarrassed."

Rebecca sucked in a breath. "Neither one had been spayed or neutered?"

Julie shrugged. "Apparently not."

"That's the real embarrassment," Rebecca said. "So what did you do?"

"I drove over to the neighbor's house and told her."

"Did they believe you?" Kate asked.

"I didn't tell them a ghost told me. I told them I worked at the vet's office and we'd run a DNA test on the dog during her last visit."

Libbie gasped. "You lied?"

Julie shrugged helplessly. "What would you expect me to do?"

"Has anyone else noticed they hear the best music in the grocery store?" Libbie asked. "I'm almost embarrassed by how much I enjoy shopping now. The other day a Duran Duran song came on and I belted out the reflex…flex flex flex." She splayed a hand across her chest. "I couldn't help myself. The teenager stacking the shelves looked at me like I was nuts."

"I've noticed myself singing along to elevator music," Julie admitted. "When did it become so catchy? I remember when it used to make me sleepy."

"That's when it was Lawrence Welk," Kate said. "Now it's the music of our generation."

"Old people music," Rebecca whispered, horrified by the

thought. "What happens when my parents get in an elevator? Do they complain about the racket?"

"They probably can't hear it," Julie joked.

"Peaches called me a Boomer and I almost choked," Rebecca said.

"I love how it's an insult now," Libbie said, smiling. "Will Gen-X be the insult for Millenials?"

"I think it already is," Kate pointed out.

With margaritas in hand, they wandered outside to bask in the glow of the moon. Rebecca felt lighter than she had in weeks. As Peaches would say, spending quality time with her friends was food for the soul.

"Does anyone else spend more money on lotion than they care to admit?" Julie asked. "I never used to be a lotion person and now I can't get enough. My skin cracks like the bottom of the Grand Canyon if I don't rub lotion all over it."

"I haven't encountered the lotion issue, but I've been doing the thing where I walk into a room and can't remember why," Libbie said. "I'll be in the middle of one task and the next thing I know, I'm standing in the pantry wondering what I'm doing there."

Julie nodded. "Same."

"I referred to a teacher as a kid the other day," Kate said in a hushed tone. "He's almost thirty."

Libbie's gaze swept the lineup of friends. "I've started taking naps in the afternoon."

"I could never do that," Kate said. "If I get in bed, that's it until the next day."

"My parents nap," Rebecca said. "And they're in bed by eight, which was handy the other night when Peter stopped by to apologize."

Three heads snapped toward her. "Wait, what?" Libbie asked.

"Why is this the first we're hearing about this?" Kate demanded.

"I've been distracted," Rebecca said. "A man isn't the center of my universe."

"Nor should it be, but we're your best friends," Kate said. "*We* should be the center of your universe."

Rebecca snickered.

"Tell us what happened," Julie insisted.

"He explained his behavior. I forgave him. We're going out again and he kissed me goodnight. In a nutshell."

Kate raised her hand for a fist bump. "There's my girl."

"And?" Julie prompted. "Don't leave out the best part. How was the kiss?"

Rebecca sighed dreamily. "Five stars. Highly recommend." She couldn't wait to do it again soon.

"I'm so happy for you," Libbie said. "You deserve all the happiness in the world."

"Like she'd take it all," Julie said. "She'd rather go without if it meant no one else could have any."

Rebecca waved her off. "I don't deserve…" She stopped herself.

*Was she seriously about to say she doesn't deserve happiness?*
*Why would she say she doesn't deserve happiness?*

There was that all-important question again—

Why?

"How's Oatmeal's eye?" Libbie asked.

Rebecca forced herself back to the conversation. "Dr. Nate says she won't regain her sight. The infection was already too advanced."

Libbie winced. "That's too bad."

"She's a survivor. I have no doubt she'll make a great companion for someone."

"There's a woman who lives at the end of our block," Kate began. "I think she could use a friend like Oatmeal."

"She lives alone?"

Kate nodded. "She has one eye too. Lost the other one in a car accident that killed her husband and son."

Rebecca grimaced. "How awful. Was that around here?" She didn't recall a local story that grim and she'd definitely remember.

"No, it happened on a highway not far outside Philadelphia. She moved here afterward. She said she was tired of people asking her how she was doing."

"I can't say I blame her," Rebecca said.

Kate swilled her margarita. "At least between them they'd have two functional eyes."

Rebecca folded her arms behind her head. "Has the woman expressed an interest in a cat?"

"I might have brought it up in a roundabout way. I think she's worried about getting attached. She doesn't want to suffer loss again."

Rebecca watched Cat-Cat wandering in the moonlight. "Why don't you invite her to come in?"

"I don't think she would. She doesn't like to drive. She orders her groceries online and rarely leaves the house."

Rebecca's stomach clenched. This poor woman was trapped by her own emotions. "Then we'll take Oatmeal to visit her. Make it seem random."

Kate's lips spread into an impressed smile. "I like the way you think."

"How's the parental visit going?" Julie asked. "Need an escape tomorrow?"

"No, I'm good, but thanks. They won't be here much longer. My dad's been telling me some good stories about my grandmother. I'm trying to remember them all."

Kate pulled a face. "I'm disappointed I haven't gotten to see them. Parents love me."

Rebecca held up her phone. "I'll show you a photo. It'll be

almost as good." She opened the photo app and started to scroll. "Here's a photo of them on the deck." Rebecca accidentally clicked on one of the videos taken during the photo shoot.

Kate laughed. "Hang on. I need to see the rest of this." She watched as Rango raced the length of the room in his superhero costume, the bearded dragon's cape flaring behind him and two cats following him from a safe distance. "What are these?"

"From the calendar photo shoot. Peaches captured the magic."

"She sure did." Kate took the phone and clicked on the next video of Meatball trying to get his head in an Uncle Sam hat. He tried all sorts of maneuvers, including rolling onto his back and sliding his head into it. Finally Dexter came along and bit the edge of the hat, flipping onto his own head and trotting away. Peaches had nearly dropped the phone at that point, she was laughing so hard.

"Rebecca, these videos are hilarious," Kate said. "You should share them on the shelter's website."

Julie wiggled her fingers. "Show me. I want to laugh too."

Kate passed the phone to her.

"I'm not sure we'd get enough traffic to matter." Rebecca figured she'd be better off uploading them to her personal Facebook profile. "Besides, people who make it as far as the website are already interested in adoption from here."

"Good point." Kate clicked her perfect oval nails on the counter. "Why don't you let me upload them on my channel as a special feature?"

Rebecca frowned. "But it's for animal adoption. Won't it confuse your subscribers?"

"Nonsense. You're a local businesswoman. Just because it's a non-profit doesn't make it any less work. If anything, it's more work."

Rebecca agreed with her on that. "Send me these videos and I'll upload them with the GoFundMe link," Kate insisted.

"Don't you already have the link on your page?"

"Yes, but it's sitting there by itself. Videos like this…" She shook her head in awe. "Trust me, this is magic. It could make a huge difference to the number of eyeballs we're getting."

"If you say so."

"We should head to Atlantic City with your gift," Libbie said, shaking an empty glass in Rebecca's direction. "We could make enough money to save the shelter *and* your retirement."

Kate cringed. "Nobody should ever head to Atlantic City for any reason. That place is like a pit of despair."

"I can't imagine the casino owners would take it well when I walk away a winner from every table," Rebecca said. "My legs might not be perfect, but I'd like to keep them unbroken."

Julie looked at her. "Did you give any thought to my casino night idea?"

Kate winked. "I'm always up for a night of competitive gambling."

Rebecca didn't want to sound ungrateful, but she was doubtful a casino night would make enough of a difference to help them reach their goal by the deadline. They didn't need poker.

They needed a miracle.

Kate's eyes sparkled with sympathy. "Stay tough. Whatever the outcome, we'll find a way to make it work. You're not alone."

Rebecca nodded. "I appreciate that." It was a good reminder for someone like Rebecca who'd felt alone most of her life.

Laughter burst from Julie and Libbie and Kate snatched the phone at the first opportunity and started tapping.

"What are you doing?" Rebecca asked.

"Sending the videos to me." Kate returned the phone to Rebecca. "There. Took a task off your plate. You're welcome."

Rebecca's gaze swept her friends and she felt herself getting choked up. It wasn't like her, but she rolled with it.

"Thank you."

## CHAPTER SEVENTEEN

THE NEXT DAY Rebecca sat at the patio table across from her parents and tried to drum up a new topic of conversation. She realized they leaned toward a bad date—superficial conversation and not many questions designed to get to know her. In her parents' case, it was probably because they assumed they already did. By this point in the visit, they'd exhausted the subject of their planned vacations for the rest of the year (Yosemite) and received the update on any living relations (Dottie has diabetes; Mona's husband has dementia). She knew which books they'd read and intended to read, which television shows they'd recently binged, and what their thoughts were on neighbors who didn't rake their leaves quickly enough to prevent them from blowing into their yard. Other than the Nonny stories, there wasn't much genuine conversation.

"This wine is nice," her mother said. She picked up the bottle to examine it. "I usually stick to California wines."

"It's a German Riesling," Rebecca said.

Her mother snapped a photo of the label with her phone. "I have this new app that keeps track of which wines I've tried and then I can rate them so I don't forget whether I liked it or not."

"Sounds handy."

"We can't remember on our own anymore," her mother said. "Can we, Vince?"

"I can't remember why I walked into the kitchen half the time," her father said.

"Usually it's to make a sandwich." Her mother bit back a smile. "Your father now considers ten-thirty in the morning an appropriate time for lunch."

"Did we tell you we're taking a cruise next year?" her father asked.

"No, you told me about the national park, but I don't think you mentioned a cruise."

Her father took a gulp of wine. "It goes all the way from Hong Kong to Vancouver."

Rebecca nearly spat her wine across the table. "Wait. You're taking a cruise across the Pacific?"

Her mother covered her father's hand with her own. "We're flying to Hong King and then sailing to Canada. Doesn't that sound incredible?"

"Thirty-seven days," her father added.

"Just the two of you?" Rebecca asked.

"No, Tom and Barb are going too," her mother said. Tom and Barb were their friends from high school. Like Rebecca's parents, they were also high school sweethearts whose marriage had endured the test of time.

"That sounds amazing," Rebecca said. It really did. She pictured herself at their age, taking a cruise across the ocean with her friends. She hoped she was half as active as her parents.

"We would've invited you, but we figure you have your own busy life here," her mother said.

No, they wouldn't have, but it was fine. Rebecca wasn't at

a point in her life where she could spend thirty-seven days on vacation. She made a mental note that such traveling opportunities existed though—her parents were experts at retirement.

"Things are hectic right now, that's for sure," Rebecca said. She heard both of their inquisitive thoughts at once— *Something's clearly going on with her* (her father). *She's a grown woman. I don't want to pry* (her mother).

"The shelter might have to close," she blurted.

Her parents exchanged concerned glances.

"Why?" her father asked. "What happened?"

She told them about Brian Shea and the sale of the building.

"That's terrible. What are you doing about it?" her father asked.

She updated them on the fundraising efforts, her searches with MaryAnn, and her meeting with Ethan.

Her mother stared at her in awe. "Your only option is to raise enough money to buy the whole building?"

Her dad whistled. "That's ballsy, Rebecca."

"It's the only good option," she admitted.

"And the hardest to achieve, I would think," her mother said. "Buildings downtown aren't going to be cheap. Your father and I have looked."

Rebecca balked. "You looked here in Lake Cloverleaf?"

"We'd considered buying a small place for the occasional weekend," her dad said. "But we ended up ruling it out. Too pricey for the number of times a year we'd use it."

"You can always stay here," Rebecca said. "I have space."

Her mother's gaze flicked to the animals' noses pressed against the glass door. "Not as much as you think. Besides, we don't want to be underfoot."

She wasn't willing to argue about the animals. This was their home as much as Rebecca's. If her parents thought they took up too much space, so be it. Still, she thought it was interesting they'd considered buying a place nearby. They seemed to lead such busy lives, which was obviously the realization they came to when they decided they wouldn't get enough use out of a Lake Cloverleaf purchase.

"More wine?" Rebecca asked.

Her mother picked up the bottle. "Why not? Nobody has to drive tonight."

"Because you're staying here and not in your own place," Rebecca pointed out.

"We would've made you drive to us," her father said. "We're getting older. Eventually nighttime driving in the mountains won't be possible for us."

Looking at her parents now, Rebecca felt like she was staring into the void. It was hard to believe there'd come a day when her parents ceased to exist. Julie was right—her parents wouldn't be around forever.

"Anybody up for a game of cards?" her father prompted.

Her parents loved playing cards. Rebecca could still remember Friday nights, falling asleep on the sofa in front of the television at Tom and Barb's house and listening to their rowdy card games as the stench of cigarette smoke penetrated her nostrils. Even now, she couldn't eat a sour cream and onion potato chip without remembering the card games. At the end of the night, she would always pretend to be asleep so her dad would carry her to the car. It was the most attention he seemed to give her and she wasn't even technically awake for it.

"I'm too tired. I think it's time for my nap," her mother said. She glanced apologetically at Rebecca. "We don't have the stamina we used to. As you've probably noticed, we're usually in bed by eight."

Rebecca held up her hands. "No judgment. I'd happily be in bed by eight if I could."

"I'm glad you told us about the shelter," her mother said. "I could tell something's been bothering you. I thought it might be relationship troubles."

If anyone else had said that, Rebecca would've assumed they were fishing for information, but she knew her mother must be genuinely curious if she cared enough to ask.

"No, I've met a nice man, but it's too soon to mention." That was as much as she was willing to share.

Her mother kissed her father's cheek before rising from the chair. "Are you coming for a nap, Vince?"

"In a minute," he said.

Her mother smiled at her. "See you in an hour or two." *She's become such an amazing woman. Vince and I got lucky with this one.*

Rebecca's heart got lodged in her throat. *Tell me that*, Rebecca urged. *Don't keep it to yourself. Share it with me.*

It occurred to her that she didn't know much about her mother's parents. They weren't around when Rebecca was growing up and she'd never thought to ask that all-important question—why? Her mother likely had her own issues that prevented her from sharing her feelings. It wasn't simply a case of not loving Rebecca the way they loved each other. It was more that they hadn't learned how to express their love for her. If they both had challenging upbringings, it was likely the parent-child bond they struggled with rather than the marital one.

She watched her mother disappear into the house. If nothing else, she was glad her parents had found each other. Maybe she, too, would be so fortunate.

Her father poured another glass of wine. "How much do you need?"

Rebecca shifted her attention back to her dad. "For what?"

"To buy the building. What would it cost?"

She flashed a grateful smile. "Dad, if you couldn't afford to buy a small place for weekends, you can't afford to buy the building."

"We own our house outright," he said. "We could mortgage it. Give you the money to buy the building." *She does so much for so many. Let me help.*

Tears welled in her eyes. Her father was offering to fix her problem. He'd never done that before. If she had a leak in her bike tire, she had to figure out how to patch it. If she scraped her knee, she knew where the bandages were in the cabinet. Yet here she was, forty-seven, and her father was offering to mortgage the family home to save the shelter—not because he loved animals—but because he loved her.

"Thanks, Dad. I won't take you up on your offer, but I appreciate it more than you know," she said.

Rebecca arrived at the shelter the next morning, feeling resigned to her fate. She'd compiled a list of shelters and would start calling them today. As tempting as her father's offer was, she couldn't accept it. Her parents were mortgage-free and advancing in age. She couldn't risk being the reason they lost their house. Even more significantly—and she didn't want to say this to him—the amount wouldn't be enough.

She checked in with MaryAnn before taking the big dogs to play in the courtyard. As she watched Paul Rudd make friends with two of the older residents, she responded to a flirty text from Peter. Who knew texting could be this enjoyable? They made plans to see each other again on Thursday night. Her parents would be gone by tonight, but she needed a few days to focus solely on preparing the shelter for closure. The thought of sending the animals to different shelters across the region upset her more than she was willing to acknowledge.

A FaceTime message appeared at the top of her phone. An incoming call from Kate? Kate never tried to FaceTime her. She reluctantly stopped texting Peter to answer the call.

"Is everything okay?" Rebecca asked.

"Where are you? I've been texting you for the past hour," Kate demanded.

"Sorry, I'm at the shelter." She didn't want to admit she'd been too focused on texting Peter to check her other messages. "What's going on?"

"Have you checked your GoFundMe today?" Kate asked.

"No. Why?"

"Do it now."

Rebecca's body suddenly felt heavy. Something was wrong. "I need to put the dogs away first. Tell me what happened."

"Brace yourself. Your story went viral."

Rebecca flinched. "In a good way or a bad way?"

"Well, you're not drunk and raging about your in-laws, so I'm going out on a limb and saying in a good way."

Rebecca resisted the urge to smile. She'd made a solemn promise never to remind Kate about her own viral video on Thanksgiving. Although the outcome had been favorable, Kate would've rather skipped the humiliation.

"You're taking too long," Kate said impatiently. "Hold on. I'll share my laptop screen."

Rebecca's eyes popped when she saw the updated number. "That can't be right. That's too many digits."

Kate smiled. "Oh, trust me. It's right."

Rebecca continued to stare at the screen in disbelief. "How?"

"People love a good animal-in-need story and you've got an entire building full of them. They've gone crazy for the videos. Meatball already has his own Twitter account and someone set up a hashtag for Cloverleaf Critters across all the social media platforms."

"I can't believe it," Rebecca murmured.

"I hope you found a printer that can handle the number of calendar orders you're going to have," Kate said. "The future's so bright, you're going to have buy sunglasses for every animal at the shelter."

They wouldn't even need the calendars if this number was to be believed. She'd do them anyway, of course, because they were going to look amazing.

Kate put herself back on the screen. "You did it, Rebecca. You saved the shelter."

Her eyes brimmed with tears. Never in her wildest dreams did she imagine the shelter would have this kind of money. She was stunned. "I couldn't have done it without you. All three of you."

"Don't give us too much credit," Kate said. "You put this in motion and stuck with it no matter how daunting it seemed."

And it *had* seemed daunting, Rebecca couldn't argue with that.

"What happens now?" Rebecca asked, still in disbelief.

"What do you think? Get that jackass Brian Shea on the phone and tell him you're about to make him an offer he can't refuse."

Except he did refuse.

Rebecca had been thrilled when Brian Shea walked through the door of the shelter. No surprise he hadn't bothered to call first. He acted like he owned the place. Okay, he did own the place, but not for much longer if she had any say in it.

"Rebecca," he'd said by way of greeting.

"Brian, I'm glad you're here." She hadn't bothered to refer to him as Mr. Shea today. Not when he insisted on calling her Rebecca. Respect worked both ways.

He'd come to let her know he'd reached an agreement with a buyer—the man she'd met called Mr. Coates.

She'd looked him directly in the eye. "How much?"

He'd appeared taken aback. "How much what?"

What she wanted to ask was how much was his soul was worth. Instead she'd asked, "How much is Mr. Coates paying for the purchase of the building?"

He'd lifted his chin and sniffed. "That's confidential. I'll expect you to have your…inventory moved by the end of the lease period. No exceptions."

"What if I offer more?"

He'd scoffed. "More what? I only accept money, Rebecca. You can't pay me in Purina."

"Is he paying the asking price? Let's see if I can beat it."

*She's completely serious. I didn't realize she was delusional.* "It doesn't matter whether you have the money or not. I have no interest in selling to you."

Rebecca stared at him. Apparently she'd been wrong. Money wasn't his primary motivator. Being a dick was.

"The whole point of you selling the building is to make money, right? If I'm willing to offer more, why not take it?"

He rested his hands flat on the counter and leaned forward. "You may recall that I own quite a few buildings in Lake Cloverleaf, Rebecca. I will be doing this community a service by removing a blight from our beautiful downtown area. Nobody wants to see rejected animals parading in and out of here on a regular basis. I'd been a fool to allow it in the first place. A spa is much more in keeping with the town's aesthetic. Quite frankly, the mayor should award me the key to the town for this act of public service."

Rebecca didn't give him the satisfaction of an outraged

response. Slowly she rose to her feet, making sure to maintain eye contact. "This blight on the town, *Brian*, provides more of a public service than anything you've ever been involved with in your life. This shelter is not a display of rejection and abandonment. The shelter is a haven of love. When you walk in here, you feel like you belong somewhere." She paused. "Not you, of course. You don't belong in a place like this full of compassion and kindness. You belong alone on an empty golf course surrounded by nothing but holes that reflect the gaping hole in your heart."

He straightened his back. "Make sure this place is thoroughly cleaned or I'll invoke the penalty fee. It reeks." He turned on his expensive heel and left the building.

Rebecca continued to stare at the door for several minutes after he left. All that fundraising had been for nothing. All the work. All the kindness on display and still Brian Shea won. Rebecca and the animals lost. It wasn't fair.

Her gaze drifted to Iago.

"No good," he squawked.

"You're right about that, my feathered friend."

After everything she'd accomplished, they would still be homeless. She started to sink into a negative headspace but stopped herself. No, wait.

She glanced at Iago. "We have one play left, Iago. In for a penny, in for a pound."

Rebecca called Charlotte Bernstein to see whether she was available to cover the shelter tomorrow. Once she arrived home, she'd say goodbye to her parents and spend the rest of the evening devising a plan.

She had everything to gain and absolutely nothing left to lose.

## CHAPTER EIGHTEEN

OTHER THAN THE odd trip to the Philadelphia airport or her parents' house, Rebecca rarely needed to drive more than thirty minutes. Everything she needed was in or around Lake Cloverleaf.

But not today.

Today what she needed was located forty-five minutes due west, where Coates Enterprises was headquartered and where she would find the one person capable of changing the shelter's fate. Her parents were gone now; she'd been pleased when they asked to return for Labor Day weekend. It was never too late to improve an important relationship. Like Kate said about relationships, both parties had a responsibility. Yes, Rebecca was their child, but she was an adult now and capable of asking for the relationship she wanted. During their brief visit, their relationship had progressed by leaps and bounds because she'd been willing to look inward as well as outward.

Rebecca blasted the radio and lost herself in the music of the 80s and 90s, grateful for the distraction. She knew what was at stake. There was no need to remind herself with each passing highway marker. She belted out the lyrics to songs by Bon Jovi, Metallica, Aerosmith, and Def Leppard. Guns N' Roses *Sweet Child of Mine* required the windows down, despite the inevitable tangles in her hair. She even suffered through an Air Supply song without changing the channel, although she had no idea how that one had slipped in among the hard rock tunes. A deejay with a sense of humor, no doubt.

Coates Enterprises was housed in a sleek office building with a shiny black exterior. The building screamed 'success.'

She parked her modest car between a Mercedes and a Lexus and opened her door carefully, easing her way out of the driver's seat. The last thing she needed right now was to clip the pricey door of a Mercedes. She certainly couldn't use the GoFundMe money for that.

As she approached the entrance, her phone pinged with a text from Peter, wishing her luck. She texted back with the crossed fingers emoji and stepped inside.

The lobby was as grand as the exterior suggested. There was even a fountain in the center that reminded her of one at the King of Prussia mall. Who knew there was such a fancy professional center so far outside the city limits?

"Can I help you find somewhere, miss?"

She approached the reception desk with a smile, grateful for the 'miss' over 'ma'am.' "My name is Rebecca Angelos and I have an appointment with Mr. Coates," she lied.

"Seventh floor," the receptionist said. He motioned to the elevator bank to her far left. "You'll take any of those three elevators and turn left when you get off on the seventh floor."

"Thank you." The heels of her sandals squeaked across the smooth floor and she hoped no one could hear them over the din of the fountain.

She stepped into the elevator and was relieved to see she

was alone. She wasn't claustrophobic, but she hated the forced intimacy of sharing confined spaces, even for a mere minute. She felt like she could hear every breath and heartbeat of the elevator's inhabitants. It was too close.

Stepping off the elevator on the seventh floor, she cleared her head and prepared for the next and final phase of Operation Save Cloverleaf Critters.

"Help me, Mr. Coates," she whispered. "You're my only hope." A *Star Wars* reference. Julie would be proud.

She pushed down on the handle to suite 705 and entered the tranquil office. Soft, sleepy music played in the background and there was a water feature in the center of the room with a few strategically placed upholstered chairs around it. Rebecca noticed a spiritual sandbox in the corner. These people took relaxation very seriously.

The woman behind the desk looked up in surprise as Rebecca entered. The lobby receptionist hadn't called ahead to alert them. Good. That gave Rebecca more time before they called security and had her escorted out. Or maybe they wouldn't. There was no way to know until she tried and she had to risk it. What was one measly smear on her record compared with the fate of the shelter?

Rebecca spotted a framed photograph of two cats on the console table behind her. A promising start.

"Can I help you?" the woman asked. "This is Coates Enterprises. If you're looking for the Altman Group, they're the next door down."

"I'm here to see Mr. Coates, actually," she said. "My name is Rebecca Angelos." She didn't apologize for her presence or ask whether he was available. She simply stated what she wanted and awaited the response.

The woman seemed uncertain. "I'm sorry, but Mr. Coates isn't available. I'd be happy to make an appointment for a later date." *Is she selling something? They know better than to let in solicitors downstairs.*

"I'm not here to sell you anything, if that's what you're worried about," Rebecca said. She glanced at the memo pad on the desk that read A Message from Cassie. "This is a business matter, Cassie."

Cassie's gaze drifted to the phone and back to Rebecca. *She seems perfectly nice, but Jason has a headache and he'll be grumpy for the rest of the day if I let this woman in there. Whatever her reason is for being here, it doesn't seem like good news.*

"If he's not expecting you, I don't see how he can fit you in today. He's a very busy man."

Rebecca debated her options. She didn't want to force her way in, but if she didn't get this meeting now…She couldn't bring herself to contemplate the remainder of the sentence.

"Do you have any pets, Cassie?"

The woman blinked. "Yes, two Abyssinian cats. Bilbo and Arwen. I wouldn't trade them for the world."

"Has Mr. Coates mentioned that the building he's in the process of buying currently houses an animal shelter?"

Cassie instinctively glanced at another framed photograph that Rebecca couldn't see, but she imagined it included the same two cats. "You mean the new Lake Cloverleaf location?"

"That's the one. I'm the director of that animal shelter, Cassie, and if Mr. Coates buys that building, the animals will have nowhere to go. Do you know what happens to animals with no prospects?"

Cassie paled and picked up the phone. "Mr. Coates, I have a Rebecca Angelos here to see you and it's urgent." She set down the phone and met Rebecca's anxious gaze. "Go right in, Ms. Angelos."

Like the reception area, the interior office was set up in a similar manner to a spa. The smell of patchouli filled her nostrils and she spotted a small waterfall in the corner of the room. The sound of running water only served to activate her bladder, but she could understand why some people found it soothing.

Jason Coates turned away from his computer and blinked in surprise. "You're the woman from the animal shelter."

"Rebecca Angelos. I'm the director of Cloverleaf Critters."

He gestured to the empty chair opposite him. "Have a seat, Ms. Angelos. Tell me how can I help you."

Rebecca explained the plight of the shelter and Brian Shea's refusal to sell the building to her, regardless of the offer. "He said he won't sell to me under any circumstances. He considers the shelter a blight on the community."

"What a tool," he remarked. A promising start.

"I understand you're a businessman and you've identified this location as being good for your spa, but it will be much easier for you to find an alternative than it will be for me. My realtor showed me a building only two blocks away that would be ideal for a spa."

He cocked an eyebrow. "But not for a shelter?"

She shook her head. "No outdoor space, which you don't need, but we do. Our needs are so specific and the shelter has spent years adapting that space to suit the animals."

"And you don't think it makes sense to take the money you presumably have for this better offer and invest it in a new building?" he asked, not unkindly. There was something soothing about Jason Coates and it had nothing to do with the waterfall or the Enya-style music playing in the background.

"Unfortunately we don't have the luxury of time, Mr. Coates. The sale is imminent. Our lease is up and the simple fact is that we have nowhere suitable to go. Believe me, if I could find forever homes for each and every one of those animals, that would be my preference, but that's not the reality we live in. And even if by some miracle we managed it, there will always be more coming through the door." The unwanted. The rejects. The abandoned. And Rebecca would be there to accept them all.

Jason licked his lips. "Do you know what drove me to have a successful business of my own?"

Her stomach plummeted. If he was about to unleash a 'bootstrap' sermon on her, she'd be out the door faster than The Flash.

"Your modest background?" she offered weakly.

He folded his hands on the desk. "I'm adopted. From a young age, I strove to be the best at everything I touched. I thought that one day my biological parents would discover what an amazing child they produced. I'd impress them so much that they'd come looking for me."

"Did that ever happen?"

He gave a mournful shake of his head. "Turns out they died when I was a toddler. I'd been chasing ghosts my whole life without knowing it."

"But you carried on building your empire," Rebecca said with a sweeping gesture.

He snorted. "Hardly an empire, but a success definitely. I love my spas, Ms. Angelos. They're a place of refuge for the weary. The stressed. The exhausted. The sick. My spas provide momentary relief from the outside world and its ills."

Rebecca couldn't argue. She loved a good deep tissue massage as much as anybody.

"But what you provide," he continued, "that is so much more important. The animals find a loving home and the people have…"

"Relief," Rebecca interrupted. "The stressed. The exhausted. The sick. Your house becomes their safe haven and they become yours."

He smiled. "Exactly. It took me many years of therapy to learn that I was good enough, with or without the acceptance of my biological parents. I didn't have to prove anything. I just had to be myself."

"Then you're way ahead of a lot of people."

They looked at each other for a long moment. She didn't need to read his mind to know he was assessing her.

Jason scratched his cheek, deliberating. "What if I sold it to you?"

Rebecca balked. "You mean you'd complete the purchase and immediately turn around and sell it to me?"

"Why else would you be here?"

"I...I thought maybe you'd back out at the last minute so he had no choice but to accept our offer."

Jason grunted. "He'd simply take it off the market and start all over again in a few months. You'd be back to square one."

Rebecca preferred his idea. Less room for error. "Are you sure about this?"

"There are more important things in the world than money."

Rebecca could hear his mind buzzing with activity. *Call the realtor and schedule a second showing of the building on Appleton Avenue. Call the lawyer.*

"This has to be our little secret," Jason continued. "If Shea gets wind of it, I doubt he'll sell to me either."

"Not a problem," Rebecca said. She'd want to hold off on the celebrations until the deed was in her hand anyway. She wasn't one to count her chickens before they hatched.

"I can have my lawyer draw up an agreement," he said. "What's your email address? I'll have it sent over as soon as it's ready."

"Don't you need to wait until the ink is dry on your own agreement?" she asked.

"It won't be an agreement of sale yet. Just something in writing to confirm our understanding. A memorandum of agreement."

She waved him off. "Don't spend your money on lawyers for my benefit. I trust you."

His eyebrows shot up. "A gentleman's agreement. I can't remember the last time I entered into one of those. Oh, that's right. Never."

"This is a woman's agreement. It's different."

His head bobbed. "It certainly is. How refreshing."

She listened to see whether he added 'and stupid' or anything else to his statement. Thankfully, she heard nothing except the words that came out of his mouth. Like Peter, the outside seemed to match the inside. Also refreshing.

"Still, I think we should have one. It protects you as much as it protects me," he said. "Do you have a lawyer who can review it for you?"

She nodded.

"I should thank you for coming here," he continued. "Your visit has given me a fresh idea."

Rebecca sat up. "For what?"

"A pet spa. My dog loves pedicures at home. I bet the animals in the area would love a bit of extra pampering."

"That sounds like a great idea," Rebecca said.

"If I wanted to hire you as a consultant, would you have time to offer input on our ideas?"

Rebecca was floored. Even with the ability to read minds, she didn't hear that offer coming. "I would be honored."

"Then it's settled. I'll sell you the building for a dollar more than I bought it for and, once I get squared away in a new location in town, we'll meet again to discuss the pet spa."

The sound of Rebecca's heartbeat thundered between her ears, drowning out any thoughts she might've overheard.

"Thank you, Mr. Coates. You're doing an amazingly selfless thing for the community."

"Nonsense. Though I don't think anyone should be doing selfless work. It's good to give back, but we all matter, don't we?"

Rebecca said a silent thank you. She felt like the universe had put Jason Coates on this earth at this precise moment in time specifically for Cloverleaf Critters. And for her.

He opened a drawer and pulled out a slip of paper. "Here's a voucher for a free spa service of your choice. Self-care is essential, in my opinion. No expiration date. Once we're up and running in the new location, I hope you'll use it."

She took the voucher and tucked it into the pocket of her purse. "You can bet on it."

## CHAPTER NINETEEN

"Congratulations," MaryAnn said, shaking her hand. "Cloverleaf Critters is now the proud owner of 132 Main Street."

Rebecca still couldn't believe she'd made this happen. She knew that if it weren't for her gift, she never would've developed the courage to go the extra mile and raise the funds they needed. The voices were less intrusive now and she found she could adjust the volume dial when necessary without the aid of the psychic hangover cure. They'd become more like white noise. The telepathy was part of her now, like all of her life experiences. She didn't leave them behind like discarded clothing. She absorbed them like vitamins and nutrients, taking the elements that benefitted her and flushing out the rest.

She arrived home to find a small cooler on her doorstep with a card attached to the lid. *Congrats* was handwritten on the envelope. Rebecca peered inside the cooler to find a bottle of champagne and a box of chocolates. Someone romantic enough to deliver champagne and chocolate but also smart enough to save them from the heat by placing them in an attractive cooler. She didn't need to read the note to know this was a gift from Peter. She tore open the envelope and scanned the contents.

*I would've preferred to deliver this in one of my handmade crates, but my pride is less important than either of the enclosed items. Hope to celebrate in person soon.*

Rebecca sighed contentedly as she lifted the cooler by the handle and carried it into the house. That Peter Putnam was a keeper.

Her phone buzzed as she set down the cooler on the kitchen counter. "Hey, Kate."

"Are you ready? We're leaving Libbie's now."

Rebecca glanced at the clock on the microwave. "Crap. I'll be ready by the time you get here. The meeting took a little longer than I thought."

"Kris Kross says jump," Julie yelled in the background.

"Jump!" Libbie added.

"We're not jumping," Kate reminded them. "This is paintball."

"I'm wearing white," Libbie said, loud enough for Rebecca to hear. "I figure I can always bleach it later if I get marks on it."

"Very sensible," Rebecca said. "Let me go so I can get ready."

She hung up and hurried around the house, letting out the dogs and refilling the food and water bowls before darting to the bedroom to get changed. Playing paintball had been another one of her ideas. She couldn't bail now.

She changed into loose shorts and a T-shirt and swapped her regular bra for a sports bra. Her boobs would thank her later.

"Let Operation Inner Child commence," Rebecca declared, as she slid beside Julie in the back seat of Kate's Land Rover.

"We picked teams," Julie said.

Rebecca slumped against the seat. "How can you have picked teams without me?"

Julie rolled her eyes. "Did you seriously think Kate and Libbie would agree to be on opposing teams?"

Libbie poked her head through the seats. "Sorry. We're a package deal. Always have been. Always will be."

"Some coven member you are," Rebecca said.

Julie looped her arm through Rebecca's. "That's okay. We'll make them rue the day they ever took up arms against us."

Rebecca cast her a sidelong glance. "Do you even know how to fire a paintball gun?"

"No clue," Julie confirmed.

"I bet Kate's been secretly practicing," Rebecca said.

Kate glanced at them in the rearview mirror. "I *may* have taken the kids to a paintball session."

"Purely for their benefit, I'm sure," Libbie added.

"Ava enjoyed the paint splatter," Kate said. "She used the opportunity to create abstract art on her brother's shirt."

"Anything qualifies as a canvas to a budding artist." Rebecca was more interested in running around like a crazy person and blowing off steam. The gym served a purpose, but it wasn't fun to walk on a treadmill or use the elliptical. Getting in touch with her inner child meant incorporating a little fun into her exercise and paintball seemed to fit the bill. She'd know soon enough anyway.

Julie glanced out the window at the passing scenery. "It's a beautiful day for shooting your friends outside."

"Not a sentence I ever expected to hear," Libbie said.

By the time they reached the paintball field, the women were raring to go. The teenager behind the makeshift counter looked past them at first, as though expecting their children to materialize.

"It's the four of us," Rebecca said.

He seemed momentarily taken aback. "Oh, I see." He glanced at the computer. "Four adults. That will be…"

"We're witches," Julie interrupted. "Paintball is one of our rituals."

He cast a wary glance at them before shifting his attention to the computer. "The cost is the same for four witches, ma'am. Are you interested in low impact or regular?"

The women exchanged glances. "Define low impact," Kate said.

"The paintballs are lighter, smaller, and slower so you don't get that sting of pain when you get hit," he explained.

Kate tossed her black American Express card on the counter. "Low impact it is."

"Oh, sorry. It's cash only," he said.

The women dug into their purses for money.

"Who carries cash anymore?" Kate complained, her nose buried in her bag.

Between the four of them, they scrounged up enough cash to play for two hours.

"I feel like I'm back in college trying to dig up beer money," Rebecca said.

"We need you to sign this waiver," the teenager said. He passed a clipboard across the counter to Kate.

"A waiver?" Libbie queried.

"It basically confirms that you're fit and healthy enough to play," he said.

"What constitutes fit and healthy?" Libbie asked.

"Do hot flashes count?" Kate asked.

"What about chronic joint inflammation?" Julie chimed in.

The women burst into laughter.

*This is so embarrassing*, the teenager thought. *It's like being trapped in a room with my mom and her friends.*

"I think we should sign the form and leave the poor kid alone," Rebecca said.

He offered a grateful smile.

The women picked up their gear from the next station and listened to the instructions.

"You're in Field A," the man said. "It's the smallest area since there's only four of you."

"How many can you fit in the other fields?" Rebecca asked.

"Up to twenty players in Field B and fifty in Field C. We've got a party coming in soon, so you got here ahead of the rush."

With their masks in place, they took their guns and tanks onto the field to prepare for battle. Rebecca had no idea what she was doing, but she didn't care. For the next two hours, she lived in the moment, hiding behind fallen logs and firing paintballs at her friends. She would definitely be sore tomorrow. Worth it.

"I've made a decision," Rebecca said between rounds. She downed another bottle of water and was grateful for the portable toilet onsite.

"About what?" Julie asked, panting with her head between her legs.

"I'm going to leave my gift to Peaches," Rebecca said.

Julie's head snapped up to stare at her, wide-eyed. "Oh. That was not the direction I thought this conversation was going to take."

Rebecca peered at her. "What did you think I was going to say?"

"I thought you'd made a decision to adopt another animal or something." Julie shrugged. "But leaving the inheritance to Peaches is nice."

"She's smart, intuitive, compassionate." The more Rebecca considered it, the more she knew she was making the right choice. "She's exactly the kind of woman who should be a witch."

"You know Ethan would be more than happy to draft the paperwork for you," Libbie said.

"I'm going to give him a call tomorrow," Rebecca said.

Kate dusted off her hands. "Is break time over? We have one more round and it's a tiebreaker."

"Someone's eager to win," Libbie said, smiling.

Kate smiled back. "Just to play. Winning isn't everything, you know."

"It's the journey, not the destination," Julie echoed.

"Any more idioms you want to throw out there before we get back to the game?" Rebecca asked.

"It's always darkest before the dawn?" Libbie suggested.

"Don't count your chin hairs before they've grown," Julie added.

"That's not a real one," Libbie said.

"No, but it should be," Julie shot back.

"Life is like a box of wine," Kate said.

Libbie looked at her friend in disbelief. "As if you would ever drink wine from a box."

Rebecca pressed her hands over her ears. "I was being sarcastic!"

"Did I tell you Paul Rudd and Simon both found a home?" Rebecca asked.

"Yes," the trio said in unison.

"Excuse me for being excited," she said. Paul Rudd had gone to live with the Morris family and Miriam had finally gotten up the nerve to adopt a cat. Simon had been the obvious choice.

"You also told us about Salem being reunited with her family and Odin finding a forever home," Kate said, mimicking her.

"Odie," Rebecca corrected her. She'd been thrilled when a

woman who'd seen the viral video had fallen in love with the unattractive dog and driven two hours to meet him. It was love at first sight.

"If that isn't the universe's way of telling you how much you matter, then I don't know what is," Julie said.

She mattered, not just to the animals in the shelter but to others and, most importantly, to herself.

*Damn right I matter*, Rebecca thought, and she realized it was the first time she'd ever told herself that. Her internal monologue finally seemed to be reflecting her outward experience.

They put on their masks and started the final round. At some point, Rebecca became vaguely aware of observers and a quick glance revealed they'd attracted the attention of another group of middle-aged women. The mothers of the party guests, most likely. Although she couldn't hear what they were saying to each other, their thoughts were on full blast.

*Have they never heard of a spa?* the mom with the sleek blonde bob thought.

*They look like children with wrinkles.*

*Lesbians, obviously.*

*How old are these women? One of them looks old enough to break a hip.*

Rebecca was tempted to ask which one, but it didn't matter. The only inner voice that mattered was her own. Smiling, she turned down the volume on the telepathy and got her head back in the game. She was having fun and not hurting anyone—well, except herself. Her lower back was going to be in spasm later, but not enough to deter her.

With Julie and Libbie now out of the final round, Rebecca had to take down Kate. She wasn't trying to cheat, but she could hear Kate's thoughts and knew exactly what her plan of attack was.

"Just you and me, Angelos," Kate called. "Who's it gonna be?"

Rebecca gathered her energy and unleashed her inner child, who was apparently very loud and violent. "Get ready to eat paint and die, Kate Golden!"

She leaped out from behind a large oak tree and fired. Red paint splattered Kate's shirt and the athletic blonde dropped to the ground with dramatic flair. Rebecca threw her arms in the air and declared victory. Compliments and congratulations poured in from her friends as they helped Kate to her feet.

"To the winner go the spoils," Kate said. She pulled two ibuprofen from her pocket and slapped them into Rebecca's outstretched hand. "Congrats. You earned it."

"I think we earned more than anti-inflammatories," Julie said. "Who wants to go back to my house for cocktails by the lake and toast to our survival?"

All hands shot into the air.

"You had me at cocktail," Rebecca said.

As her friends gathered their belongings and prepared to vacate the premises, Rebecca gave the field a final sweeping glance. She'd survived more than a paintball game. Sure, she had scars, but who didn't? It was impossible to experience life without struggle or injury. The important part was to rise up and ask—what can I learn from this? Rebecca had taken the unwanted gift of telepathy and made it the best thing that ever happened to her. Inga would approve.

Rebecca glanced at her friends, walking arm-in-arm ahead of her. They didn't look particularly tough. To the untrained eye, they looked like any random middle-aged women you might see in Costco or Target.

But they were so much more than that. Every woman was so much more than what the naked eye could possibly perceive.

After everything the universe had thrown at the four of them, they were still standing. Still learning. Still growing.

Life was like a cart of cocktails—sometimes neat, sometimes stirred or shaken, or on the rocks. And in the case of Rebecca and her magical friends...

With a twist.

\* \* \*

To learn more about my books and keep up with new releases and sales, please join my newsletter via my website at www.annabelchase.com.

Other series by Annabel Chase
- The Bloomin' Psychic
- Spellbound/Spellbound Ever After
- Starry Hollow Witches
- Federal Bureau of Magic
- Crossroads Queen
- Midnight Empire
- Magic Bullet
- Hex Support Mysteries
- Pandora's Pride
- Spellslingers Academy of Magic
- Demonspawn Academy
- Divine Place

Made in United States
Cleveland, OH
11 January 2025